*For all the girls*

# *Chapter 1*

'I ate my feet!'

Harriet took a moment to work out what Marianne meant. Marianne was sitting on the floor in the big, airy studio, stretching her feet back and forth doing 'good toes, naughty toes'; regarding them in the huge mirror with a ferocious frown. Light suddenly dawned on Harriet. 'Hate!' She meant 'hate', not 'ate'. Even though they'd been friends for two years now, Harriet still found Marianne's accent confusing sometimes. Her English wasn't bad but she couldn't manage 'w's and 'th's, and 'h's were non-existent.

'There's nothing wrong with your feet,' said Harriet. 'I keep telling you. There's nothing wrong with you at all.'

She gave an inaudible sigh and avoided looking at herself, twizzling round on her bottom away from the mirror to make sure. Mirrors, mirrors, all around.

She sat hugging her knees, her shoulders slumped. Why did it have to matter what shape you were, as long as you could dance?

'But look at *your* feet, 'Arry.'

Harriet looked down at them. They were the best thing about her: high insteps, strong arches, good workaday feet for a dancer. But when she looked at Marianne: tiny, slim, long legs, neck like a – a swan, there was no other word for it. And her feet were good enough for anyone except herself. Harriet gave another sigh.

'There is nothing wrong with your feet, Marianne,' she said again, emphasizing each word. 'Nothing wrong at all with any bit of you.'

Like almost everyone in the school, Marianne never stopped worrying about what she looked like, but since the assessments three weeks ago, Harriet suddenly realized, she seemed to have got worse. Marianne gave a French kind of shrug and pouted a bit. Then she smiled.

'Oh 'Arry, always you say the right thing.'

She leapt up and spun round in front of the mirror, landed in a perfect fifth position and examined herself in the mirror, turning her head, poking and prodding at bits of herself, rising and lowering on the offending feet, the instep not exactly bulging but more than enough for most people. Most dancers. The frown returned as she began to experiment with her turn out.

The studio door banged open and Gareth strode in, his ballet bag hoiked over one shoulder.

' 'Ullo, 'Arry,' he said with a grin, mimicking Marianne's accent. He hopped over Harriet's legs, dumped his bag in the corner, levered off his trainers toe to heel, tied his sweatshirt round his waist and flopped down beside her to put on his soft-shoes. But all the while, Harriet noticed without surprise, he didn't take his eyes off Marianne.

'Bonjour, toi,' he called out to her.

Marianne chasséed out of the classiest arabesque Harriet had seen in a long while and came over to him, her pointe shoes making her waddle with her weight back on her heels. She placed a hand on his shoulder and kissed the air on either side of his cheeks, dipping forward and tossing up a nonchalant leg vertically behind her.

'Ga-a-arette,' she said in a singsong voice, and returned to surveying herself critically in the mirror, her fluffy white practice tutu sticking out round her, making her legs look even longer. 'I lo-o-ve pas de deux class. Pas de deux,' she hummed to herself, 'is best.'

She swung into a spectacular pirouette. Gareth looked at Harriet.

'What *shall* we do with her?' he said with a grin.

'Nothing, *Garrette*,' said Harriet. 'She'll do very well for herself, without us doing anything.'

'True,' said Gareth, with a glum little nod, 'but it would be nice to be noticed once in a while.'

'Nutter!' said Harriet. 'Of course she notices. You know she does. She's just – just – well, if you're going to dance you've got to be single-minded, you know that. And she's single-minded.'

'Hmm,' said Gareth. 'I sometimes think I'm just good for being her pas de deux partner. Marianne's crane,' he said, sticking up an arm above his head with a rueful shrug.

Harriet laughed. 'Oh, go on,' she said. 'You know it's not like that. It's just that she knows what she wants and works for it. She's got her priorities right, I suppose you could say.'

Gareth gave her knee a friendly pat. 'And you don't? Come on, Harry.'

'Look,' said Harriet, keeping her voice low, 'we all know where she's going. To the top . . . to the very, very top. You just have to watch her for five minutes and you know.'

'Yep,' said Gareth with a smile that managed to

look proud of Marianne and a little sad all at the same time. 'She'll be up there with the greats, you're right. And then . . .'

'And then you'll be up there with her, Gareth. You will. You won't get left behind. They as good as told you that at the assessments.' Gareth gave a modest shrug. Harriet hesitated. 'But me . . . well . . .'

Harriet's tone made Gareth suddenly look concerned.

'What do you mean? You're a *very* good dancer, Harry.'

'Mmm. But not quite good enough.'

'Plenty good enough. You're strong and quick – punchy, and you can jump like . . .'

'But not quite the right – the right *shape*. Short and squat, me.'

'No, you're not.'

'Yes, I am. Well, compared with some.' She nodded in the direction of Marianne, but with no malice in her glance. 'Anyway . . . it appears I'm not "company material".' She made a face, rolling her eyes, and lowered her head on to her knees for a moment. 'I kind of knew ages ago really, but after the assessment . . .'

Gareth burst out: 'Is that what they told you? And you've been keeping it to yourself all this time? I hate those assessments. They do more harm than good, if you ask me.'

'No. They tell it how it is, Gareth.'

'But—'

'But nothing. Honest. They just made it clear.' She made quotation marks in the air with her fingers. ' "You're a capable dancer, Harriet my dear, a little shall-we-say overenthusiastic at times perhaps, but just not quite what we are looking for *physically*, you understand, so . . ." Anyway, I only have to look in the mirror . . .'

'You're not going to give up?'

' 'Course not. And I haven't got to leave or anything. I mean, I can finish the training but then . . .'

'Oh, Harry, that's – that's just . . .'

'There's other things to do but join this company, Gareth – let's face it, who wants to be thirty-sixth swan for ever? Not likely.'

Quite what those other things might be, she wasn't sure yet, but she was equally sure that she would find out somehow. Gareth looked at her, a troubled frown on his face, his hand, absent-mindedly, still on her knee. She lifted it off, plonked it down on his own and scrambled to her feet as Miss McGregor came in with the pianist. Gareth glanced over at Marianne and Harriet noticed his face soften.

The students moved to the barre, adjusting garments, flexing muscles. Harriet went over to where Marianne had already chosen her spot, one leg up round her ear somewhere. Harriet grinned at her, shook her head and, leaning forward, both hands on the barre, stretched the back of each leg alternately, bouncing gently up and down. She pushed the practice tutu down firmly over her hips and eased herself into second position for the first plié. The pianist settled himself and ran his fingers quickly up and down the keyboard, as Miss McGregor gave a brief smile round the room, clicked her fingers '. . . and two, and three, and four, and . . .' The class began.

Afterwards, Harriet's partner, Will, wanted to practise a lift that had gone wrong. Gareth followed Marianne out of the studio. By the time Harriet got to the canteen, they were sitting together at a table. In front of him, Gareth had a sandwich and a cup of tea, two Mars bars and a packet of crisps. Marianne, pointe shoes on the table, was sipping at a Diet Coke. Harriet fetched an egg salad and a yoghurt from the bar and went to sit with a group of other girls, but Marianne called her over.

' 'Arry! Where are you going?'

'Thought you might want to be alone,' said Harriet with a grin, looking at Gareth. He shoved out a chair for her to sit next to him.

'Don't be daft,' he said with a slight frown, looking at Marianne under his eyebrows. Marianne paid no attention but went on sipping her Coke, stirring the straw round in the neck of the bottle. She looked up at Harriet.

'You get it right, 'Arry?'

'What? Oh, the lift you mean. Well, sort of. I expect it's my fault, but I can't quite see why it doesn't work really properly yet. Will's a hero anyway, taking me on.'

She dug into the salad, spearing a tomato and demolishing it. Marianne reached over, extracted a bit of lettuce and started to nibble.

'Help yourself,' said Harriet, pushing the plate a bit nearer Marianne, but Marianne shook her head and wriggled back in her seat.

'What do you mean, Will's a hero?' said Gareth.

'Well . . . lumping me round like he does,' said Harriet, cutting the egg and embellishing it with mayonnaise. 'Like carting round a sack of potatoes.'

'Oh, come on, Harry, anyone would think you weighed a tonne.'

'Not far off,' said Harriet cheerfully, avoiding his eyes.

'Well, I can lift you, easy.'

'Yeah? Anyway, it doesn't matter any more. No *Rose Adagio* for me, mateys. I'm just sorry for Will, that's all, while I'm still here.'

Marianne sat forward. 'What? I don't understand. Why do you say that?'

Gareth sighed. 'Harry's got the idea she's not going to dance.'

Marianne looked horrified. 'But . . .'

'That's not what I said at all,' said Harriet, polishing off the mayonnaise with a bit of roll. 'I said not with the company, that's all. There are other places, you know. Places where you don't have to be just the right height, just the right shape, just the right – I don't know – right everything . . . Where you don't have to starve to death to . . .' She gave a quick look at Marianne but there was no reaction. She tore the lid off the yoghurt, shifted Marianne's shoes and the Mars bars, hunting about on the table, then stood up and bounced across the canteen to fetch a spoon.

'Oops,' said Gareth.

'She is upset,' said Marianne.

'Just a bit, you could say.'

'But she wants to dance. She cannot give up, Garette, non.'

'They've told her she won't get into the company. Last assessment. She just told me. I didn't know. Did you?'

Marianne frowned, looked round at Harriet and shook her head. 'She did not tell me . . .'

'Nor me. She's kept it to herself—' Gareth stopped suddenly as Harriet returned, hooked the seat underneath her with her foot and sat down. She dug the spoon into the yoghurt.

'Mmm,' she said, sucking the spoon vigorously, 'not bad, but just think – if you didn't have to watch it all the time, you could have ice cream, and banana and custard and – and . . .'

'Mars bars?' said Gareth, pushing one towards her.

Harriet put out her hand, then drew it back with a rueful smile.

'Not yet,' she said, 'give me time. I'm not used to the idea yet. I've lived on a diet for two whole years. And let's face it, I'll always have to be careful, I suppose, no matter what I do. Careful. Sensible. What a life.'

'You wouldn't swap it, you know you wouldn't,' said Gareth and she laughed.

'Maybe not,' she said, 'we'll have to see.'

'Crème brulée,' said Marianne suddenly, with a faraway look in her eyes.

Gareth laughed. 'Can't oblige with that,' he said. 'Here, you have the Mars bar.'

'Non, non, non,' said Marianne, waving her hands and shaking her head frantically, 'mustn't even think – chocolate . . . no. I can feel my 'ips growing just looking at it.'

Gareth laughed again, but bit his lip.

'You can finish my yoghurt if you like,' said Harriet. 'That won't hurt you.' She gave Marianne another quick look from the corner of her eye.

Marianne peered into the little pot, ran a finger round the edge and put it in her mouth. For a moment or two, she chewed on it. Eyes wide, she peered in again, looked up at Harriet and said, 'Doesn't count, does it, if it is someone else's?'

She went to put in her finger again but snatched it away looking guilty, picked up her things hastily, stuffed her shoes into her bag and stood up.

'See you later,' she said. 'Repertoire, 'alf past four?'

Kissing the air towards each of them, she clattered across the canteen in her clogs and disappeared through the door.

Harriet scratched her head. 'Now you see her, now

you don't,' she said. 'Comes of being a Swan Queen in the making, I suppose.'

'Yup,' said Gareth. 'I suppose you're right.' He hesitated, fiddling about with his empty sandwich carton. 'Harry . . .' he said, looking up at her quickly then looking away again. 'Do you . . . I mean, do you ever see her eat? I mean, actually eat?'

Harriet sighed. 'No, I don't, well – herb tea, black coffee, Diet Coke . . . But, Gareth, she must eat some time. She's got the strength of an ox for all she's so – so skinny. That's got to come from somewhere. Oh, she's so lucky. I think she could eat a herd of horses – chocolate ones – and never put on an ounce. And here's me been dieting ever since I got here and look at me . . .'

'I'm looking and you're fine. And you don't starve, you eat – sensibly. But Marianne . . . Look, Harry, I know dieting's a habit round here, even a couple of the boys are at it, but . . .'

'Yes, I know, there's dieting and – and dieting. I had noticed, Gareth, but I suppose I just hoped it wasn't happening. What do you think we should do?'

But before Gareth could answer, there was a noise in the corridor, upraised voices, scuffling. Gareth jumped up and swore under his breath.

'If that's Jessica again, I'll . . .'

The door opened and Jessica stormed in. Heads turned and looked up at her as she hitched up her leotard strap over her shoulder and shook herself.

'What's up, Jess?' said a voice, with what might have been a suppressed laugh.

'Nothing,' she said, making an effort to breath evenly. 'Nothing I can't handle.'

'I'll bet,' said the voice, and a giggle ran round the room. Jessica joined a group at a far table, and immediately, two or three immaculately groomed heads drew together in sympathy with the still scarlet-faced girl.

Just then, Will barged in, letting the doors swing behind him. He stuck out his bottom to stop them, launched into a series of chassés pas de bourrés across the room, ending with a slide on to Harriet's table. He ran his fingers through his dark curls – highlighted today with pink – spiking them up into a quiff.

'Was that Jessica having a go at Marianne out there?' said Gareth.

Will nodded, casting his eyes at the ceiling with a theatrical sigh.

'They had a bit of a *do* in the corridor. One of Jessica's mates put her up to it, I think, but you know what Marianne is . . . she won't let go once the bit's between her teeth. Grrr!' He bared his own teeth and shook his head, crooking up his fingers like claws.

'Huh,' said Gareth. 'Why can't they just leave her alone?'

'You know why not,' said Will. 'Because lousy Jessica was the Big Fromage before Marianne came and she can't handle it.'

'But they're so different,' said Gareth. 'I can't see why Jessica doesn't realize there's room for both of them.'

Harriet couldn't either, but the place was full of petty rivalry and bitching. One minute you had a best friend, the next you didn't – though at least she and Marianne had lasted. But Jessica was a prize freak when it came to being jealous and she'd say anything to Marianne to upset her.

'She's in training for Queen of the Wilis, she is,' said Will with a pert nod towards Jessica. 'Beaky nose, pointy fingernails, purple lippie and all.' He pouted, making a juicy kissing sound with his lips. 'Bet she'll do Queen of the Wilis one day. Superbaddie in *Giselle* bossing all those poor wimpy little maidens – she's made for it.'

He pulled himself up on to the half pointe in a tight, tight fifth position, twirling round in a circle with tiny steps, both hands crossed at the wrists under his chin, mouth pursed, eyes narrowed in a wicked look. Then he whipped into a spiky arabesque, fingers pointed, wrists dropped, and tossed his head.

'Oh, Will, you're evil,' said Harriet, laughing, 'that's so-o-o Jessica! Queen of the Wilis to a T.'

But Gareth only raised a slight smile. He sat leaning on his arms folded in front of him on the table, his mind on Marianne.

*Chapter 2*

In the cloakroom, Harriet found Marianne hunched up on a bench, her back to the wall, feet pulled up under her, coats and bags dangling round her ears. The room smelt of old shoes and disinfectant, thinly disguised with deodorant and soap from the showers. These were the other side of an archway, through which steam filtered, making the tiled floor damp and the mirrors fog over.

Harriet hung up her practice tutu and sat next to Marianne to take off her shoes.

'What's the matter?'

Marianne shook her head and shrugged.

'There's something. It's – it's not just Jessica, is it? What is it?'

Harriet wound the ribbons round her shoes carefully, not looking at Marianne. Out of the corner of her eye she saw her roughly brush her hand across her eyes.

'She say – said I'm fat.'

Harriet let out a hoot of laughter. 'You're joking! Oh come on, Marianne. She's just trying to get to you. How many times have I got to tell you, you are *not* fat. Anything but.'

'My 'ips, she said.'

Harriet jumped up and wiped off a mirror with her sleeve. It dripped a little and the reflection of her own face was blurred, so she went into a cubicle next door and tore off some toilet paper. Vigorously and with some muttering about 'lousy Jessica', she polished the mirror till it shone brighter than it had for many a month.

'Now,' she said fiercely, 'come and look here.'

She grabbed Marianne by the arm and made her stand up.

'Your hips,' she said, 'your hips are – are *perfect*. No lumps, no bumps, just perfect. You can even see the . . . see the bones . . .'

She faltered. Marianne tried to wriggle from her grasp but Harriet renewed her hold and made her stand there.

'Look at mine if you want to see hips,' she said. She looked at herself, then at Marianne. She felt suddenly uneasy about Marianne's bones. For a moment she almost preferred her own smooth, rounded shape: not fat, nor yet a swan by any means, but not sticking out like – like that . . . She looked away and swallowed. Like lots of the other students Marianne was covered in baggies most of the time and she hadn't noticed . . . Had those bones always been like that, or had things got worse than she'd thought?

'Listen, Marianne,' she said, 'you don't have to worry about anything. You've got everything going for you.'

'But the Director said – 'e said I must watch my figure.'

'At the assessments?'

Marianne nodded. Harriet sniffed. Perhaps Gareth was right about those awful assessments. Perhaps they did do more harm than good.

'Really, is that exactly what he said?'

Marianne dropped her eyes. 'Something like that.'

'Hmm. Well . . . something like that, or exactly like that?'

Marianne didn't answer but just looked miserable.

'But, Marianne, they – the staff I mean – they say that to everyone. It's staff-speak, just what they *always* say. Doesn't matter who to. What do you think he said to me, for goodness sake? And as for Jessica –

don't take any notice of her. I tell you, she's just winding you up.'

'Why? I did nothing to 'er.'

'You didn't have to do anything. You're just very, very good, that's all. Like Will said, she used to be the Big Fromage and now she's afraid she's not.'

Marianne broke into a smile. 'Oh, 'Arry,' she said, 'that's not 'ow you pronounce fromage. Your accent is affreux – terrible.'

'Ooo là,' said Harriet with a mock toss of her head, glad Marianne's mood was broken. 'Just as well I'm not doing French, then, isn't it? Here . . .'

They sat down on the bench and she took a couple of peppermints from her bag.

Marianne frowned. 'I don't like . . .'

'Yes, you do,' said Harriet firmly. 'You drink that peppermint tea sometimes. I've seen you. Just eat it, will you?'

Meekly, Marianne took the sweet, licked it a couple of times, popped it in her mouth and crunched it up. Suddenly, she put out a hand and took another and another and another, cramming them all in at once.

Harriet grinned. 'That's better,' she said. 'Here, you might as well have the last one.' She took it out and shoved it into Marianne's already full mouth. Marianne giggled and spluttered and Harriet laughed. She blew up the empty sweet bag and burst it with a bang, crumpled it up and lobbed it into the bin.

'There,' she said, 'that's what I think of lousy Jessica. Rubbish. Come on. We've got an hour till next class and I'm behind with my English project. Let's go up to the library. You've got stuff to do, haven't you?'

'OK. I suppose I should look at my biologie.' Marianne started foraging in her bag. 'Oh zut – I must 'ave left it . . . I'll catch you up,' she said.

'What are you looking for?'

'My sweatshirt.'

'Here it is,' said Harriet, 'right in front of your eyes,' and she pulled it down from the peg above her head and waved it at her.

Marianne hesitated. 'Oh . . . er, well, I need to go to the . . .' She nodded towards the toilets next door. 'I'll catch you up . . .' she said again.

'I'll wait for you, it's OK,' said Harriet.

'No, I – er . . .' Marianne looked embarrassed. 'Go ahead, 'Arry. I'll come up in a minute.'

'Oh, all right,' said Harriet. 'See you upstairs.'

Outside the cloakroom, she paused. Why did Marianne want to be left on her own like that? A nasty thought suddenly pushed itself into her head.

Those peppermints . . . Marianne surely wasn't going to *throw up* because of them, was she? Harriet shook her head impatiently. Half a dozen peppermints, little ones? That was ridiculous. Of course she wouldn't. Feeling suddenly guilty about her suspicions, she set off up the corridor just as Gareth was coming out of the boys' cloakroom. Harriet stopped, the feeling of unease coming back.

'What's the matter, Harry?'

'I – oh, nothing.'

Quietly, she went back to the girls' cloakroom door, pushed it open and listened. Nothing.

Gareth came up to her. 'What's wrong?'

'It's just that . . . well . . .' and she told him about the peppermints, what Jessica had said about Marianne being fat, and what the Director had said too.

'I'm worried about her,' said Gareth. 'You are too, aren't you?'

'I am now,' said Harriet. 'I mean, I thought I might be imagining things and – and I didn't *want* it to be true – you know? But now you've noticed it as well . . .'

Gareth eased open the cloakroom door again and listened. 'I can't hear anything.'

'The toilets are round the corner through the arch;

we might not be able to hear from here,' said Harriet.

'If she's started throwing up, we've really got a problem.'

'We don't know that she is. But – should we talk to someone? Somehow, I just can't talk to her about it. She just sheers off it for one thing, except for going on about how fat she is.'

'Maybe I'll have a go,' said Gareth, 'but I'll have to be careful. For one thing, you're right, we don't know for certain, and if the Director did tell her to watch her weight, maybe . . . maybe he knows best . . .' He shrugged, his face anxious.

'They tell everyone to watch their weight,' said Harriet angrily. 'We're all supposed to be like – like . . .'

'Sylphs?' said Gareth with a rueful smile.

'Wilis more like. Little dead maidens that come out at midnight in the graveyard,' said Harriet, remembering the hip-bones in the mirror. 'But, Gareth, I don't want to make trouble for her if there's no need.'

'Let's just keep an eye on her for a while till we're sure,' said Gareth. 'Watch it, here she comes.'

The door opened and Marianne came out of the cloakroom. Harriet looked at her. She seemed all right. Nothing untoward. She wasn't wiping her mouth. She didn't look ill, simply surprised that Harriet was still there.

'I – er, I met Gareth,' said Harriet a little awkwardly.

Marianne nodded. 'Yes, I see,' she said with a smile. 'OK. You still want to go to the library?'

'Yes,' said Harriet. 'My project's sitting there waiting and it won't do itself.'

'See you later, then,' said Gareth.

Harriet picked up her bag. Together, she and Marianne went up the long, elegant staircase that wound up to the second floor, the slap of their footsteps echoing up the stairwell. Below them, the sounds of pianos battled with each other across the wide hallway from studio to studio, and laughter came from one of the schoolrooms on the first floor where ordinary lessons took place. More than half their time was spent dancing, but maths and biology and English and everything else had to be fitted in too. 'You're not just a pair of pretty legs and feet,' the Director said over and over again. 'You need a brain that works as well.'

Harriet sometimes wondered if most of the other students ever took that in. From the way they carried on, dance, dance, dance, and particularly ballet, ballet, ballet, was all they ever thought about. But she enjoyed her other lessons and anyway, the best thing, she thought, was to get on with them so the teachers had no reason to nag.

Inside the library, it was suddenly quiet. Most of the chairs with their wooden arms and red leather seats were empty. They chose a table together, got out pens and folders, and Harriet went to a pigeonhole where her reserved books were waiting. She spread them on the table and Marianne moved her chair nearer, kneeling up on one knee to look over Harriet's shoulder.

'What are you doing?' she said. 'I forget.'

'The first *Coppélia*,' said Harriet. 'You, of all people, should remember that. It was in France, in Paris. 1869 it was.'

'Yes?'

'Didn't I tell you? I'm sure I did.'

'Maybe. I forget. I don't like 'istory too much.'

'But it's interesting. Honestly. Look, I'll show you.'

Harriet took one of the books and opened it at a page of photographs of ballet-dancers from the time of the first *Coppélia*. Round, plump-cheeked faces looked out at them, some with sausage curls gathered in the neck, others with outlandish headdresses that looked as if they weighed a tonne. The men wore handlebar moustaches and quaint hairstyles plastered down across their foreheads, one with a kiss-curl. Marianne squinted down at them, wrinkling her nose.

'Quelle horreur!'

Harriet looked at her. 'They're not horrible. They're different but . . .'

'Non, non. Look 'ow fat they are. That girl there, look . . .'

'It's just the dress that makes her look like that.'

'But 'er legs . . . and 'is, there, look. Mon Dieu, look at the legs.'

Harriet laughed. She had to admit that the legs, especially the men's, were a bit, well . . . chubby. They looked as if they had been blown up with bicycle pumps. No bones, no bones at all.

'They are all soft and squashy.' Marianne wrinkled her nose again.

'You mean if you sat on them, they'd be like nice cosy sofas. Y-e-e-es, but the fashion was different then. And when you read about them, I think they could really dance. After all, they did lots of the ballets we still do nowadays, and we think they're difficult enough. And the book tells you about some of the steps they could do, cabrioles and fouettés and stuff . . .'

'No, 'Arry. I don't believe it. Look at this

arabesque,' said Marianne in a disgusted tone. 'No line – no – no feeling for the stretch . . . no strength . . . arms like cotton wool . . . pfffff!'

She turned the page and burst into giggles at a picture of a stocky little man in a tight jerkin with a skirt that came almost to his knees, his hair parted in the middle in big waves down to his podgy cheeks, his calves bulging out of long boots. He was leaning forward, looking into the distance, blowing on a curled hunting horn.

'Imagine – to dance with 'im,' she said.

'I know. He does look pretty daft,' said Harriet, 'but he looks strong. I bet he could lift you—' She cut herself off quickly. What a stupid thing to say with Marianne the way she was. 'I mean, not *you* you. I mean anyone . . . those girls back then . . . I think the little kids in the first year could lift you.'

She drew a quick breath, but Marianne had apparently not registered what she had said and was still turning the pages.

'They don't look so 'orrible in their ordinary clothes. Long dresses that cover them up, you know. Who is she?'

She pointed to a dark-haired woman in a floor-length, off-the-shoulder gown in ruched taffeta covered in black lace. Small eyes in a plain face stared out of the photograph, head slightly tilted to one side, one hand held across a small waist encircled in a wide, stiff belt.

'Madame Dominique,' read Harriet. 'Oh, I know who she was. I've read about her. She was a teacher at the Opéra.'

'L'Opéra? À Paris? Ah, chouette!' Marianne grabbed the book and looked more closely.

'That's where they all were,' said Harriet. 'That's what I was trying to tell you.'

'All of them danced à l'Opéra? In Paris?'

Harriet nodded. 'Well, I think so, though not the opera house that's there now. That one was built in the 1870s, I think – I haven't got to that bit yet. I think there was another one, much older, that burnt down. The girl I'm researching was dancing in the old building, before the fire happened. Madame Dominique was her teacher.'

'What girl?'

Harriet took the book and turned a few pages. She held out a page with a black and white photograph of a young girl with dark hair piled on top of her head, a few ringlets tumbling down her neck. She knelt on one knee, her slim, white hands crossed in front of her, her white tulle skirts frothing out round her with one little foot showing beneath them. The tiny frills on the bodice of her costume displayed pale, sloping shoulders and a long neck round which hung a fine chain carrying a cross. A spray of leaves decorated her hair and a trail of leaves ran from her waist to the hem of her dress. Her eyes were lowered modestly, looking down serenely at a bouquet of flowers on the floor in front of her.

'Ooooh,' said Marianne, 'mais, elle est – ah, she is beautiful.'

'Her name is Giuseppina,' said Harriet with a proprietorial little smile. 'That's who I'm researching. Giuseppina Bozzacchi. She was the first ballerina to dance Swanilda in *Coppélia*. 1869, I told you . . . They made the whole ballet on her, right from scratch. It's such a difficult role and you have to make it look so easy – it has to look *fun* . . . and just think, Marianne, she was only sixteen. Not much older than us.'

'Tell me about 'er. Why 'as she got an Italian name if she danced in Paris?'

'I don't know any more yet. I told you I had work to do,' said Harriet with a smile.

Marianne riffled through a few more pages. 'Look, 'ere she is again. Aaaah!'

'Now what's the matter?'

'She is on pointe, but she's resting 'er elbow on this . . .' She jabbed a finger at the photograph. 'Look, she need to 'old on to balance. She can't stand on pointe on 'er own. Oh là!'

Harriet looked. The girl was indeed balancing with her elbow on a piece of scenery like a balustrade on a balcony. She looked out of the photograph with big, dark, grave eyes, her curls touching her shoulder.

'It took ages to take a photograph in those days,' said Harriet. 'I remember my dad told me once – he likes old photographs. He said everyone had to be sort of propped up with a thing behind your neck to keep you still, even if you were sitting down. And I guess if you were on one leg it would be impossible without something to lean on – and look, she hasn't even got proper pointe shoes. They didn't have them then.'

'No pointe shoes? Then 'ow . . . ?'

'They darned ordinary soft-shoes and padded them with cotton wool. They weren't hard like ours. But they were so light on their feet they just sort of, well – went up on their toes. You know, really lifted up and – up they went. I've seen you do it, sometimes.'

'Not for a whole ballet,' said Marianne, 'not even for a whole enchaînement. But, 'Arry, they can't have been fat at all. Really, really thin. Not to 'ave pointe shoes and still to go up on pointe like that for a whole ballet – I couldn't do that.'

She turned away, running her hands over her stomach and muttering in French. Harriet understood bits of it, mostly about how light you'd have to be to couru for instance, or to pirouette with no pointe shoes. After a moment, Marianne sat down and pulled the book towards her, studying it intently.

'Gi-u-seppina,' she crooned. 'Gi-u-seppina. She is taking 'er call. The bouquet is to show 'ow well she 'as danced. 'Ow brilliant. One day, one day, that will be . . .' Her voice trailed away, as she studied the photograph of the girl kneeling down with her head lowered towards the flowers on the floor.

Suddenly, Marianne stiffened. Slowly, her eyes widening, she pushed the book away. For a moment she sat frozen, her arms stretched in front of her, staring at it. Then she started to shake. She slammed the book down hard, pushed back her chair and rushed out of the room.

'Marianne! Marianne, what's the matter? What's wrong?'

Harriet leapt to her feet, as the teacher in charge of the library came into the room and stood looking back after Marianne. The teacher turned to Harriet.

'Hush, Harriet. This is a quiet room, you know.'

'But—'

'If there's something wrong, you should go after Marianne, but don't make a noise here, please.'

Harriet quickly gathered up her things and reached for the book. It had fallen open at the photograph of Giuseppina kneeling down. She frowned. There was something not right. Something . . .

She thought for a moment and gently touched the photograph with one finger. Hadn't the young dancer been facing the other way when they had looked at her first? Giuseppina was facing to the left then, but now . . . now she was facing to the right.

*That's nonsense*, thought Harriet. *It's a photograph in a book. I must have remembered it wrong.* She closed the book and paused. Marianne had been pretty jittery about something. Maybe she was ill. Better go and find out what was wrong.

As she put the book back in the pigeonhole, Harriet held on to it for a moment. She gave a little shiver. Suppose – suppose the girl in the photograph *had* turned the other way . . . ? She pushed the book firmly away from her. No. It wasn't possible. There must be something else bothering Marianne. She picked up her bag and hurried from the room.

# Chapter 3

Voices babbled up the stairwell as Harriet padded down after Marianne.

'Paris!'

'Do we all get to go?'

'Paris Opéra? That's really big stuff.'

'I bet it's just some studio performance somewhere.'

'No, look, it's for real. Paris Opéra.'

Harriet took the stairs two at a time and joined the crowd jostling round the notice-board in the main hall. She balanced on the tips of her trainers to peer over the heads and shoulders pressing forward in front. Someone gave her an unlucky shove and she nearly went flying, but she grabbed a convenient arm, righted herself and burrowed between the bodies straining to see the large sheet of pink paper on the board.

'Performance at the Opéra de Paris,' it read. 'The

school has been invited to give a matinée performance early next month at the Opéra de Paris. A limited number of students will be involved in this performance and will be notified shortly. The programme will include excerpts from *Swan Lake* including the Dance of the Little Swans, a divertissement of demi-caractère dances from various ballets and a new Alistair Mildmay pas de deux.'

Alistair Mildmay was a brilliant young choreographer just beginning to make a name for himself. He had come in to one or two pas de deux classes to work on a few ideas, and afterwards, each time, the place had hummed with excitement.

*He'll want to use Marianne*, thought Harriet at once. She looked round. Marianne was nowhere to be seen, but Gareth was standing at the back of the crowd. She wriggled through to him.

'That'll be you and Marianne,' she said, 'the new pas de deux. He really liked you both when he came in to class that time.'

Gareth tried looking modest but only managed a grin. 'Hope so,' he said, 'but it could be Jess and Peter or even Jess and Will, maybe.'

Harriet shook her head firmly. 'Don't think so. Jessica wasn't too good at all those tricksy little lifts he likes. Peter couldn't really manage her . . . and Will's strong enough but he's hardly ever danced with her. He's always been lumbered with me, poor thing. It'll be you and Marianne, I bet.'

Gareth glanced round at the crowd that by now was beginning to thin out. 'Where is she?'

'Don't know.' Harriet frowned. 'She ran out of the library a while ago. She looked really upset about something. I was just going to look for her when I saw that.' She nodded at the notice-board.

'Upset? Why?'

Harriet shrugged. 'One minute she was looking at my book of photos of olden-day dancers, the next minute she slammed it down and legged it. She looked really . . . well, shaken up, somehow.'

'You don't think . . . ?'

Harriet met his eyes, then looked away. 'What, back to the toilets, you mean?' she said slowly. 'Oh, Gareth, please not . . .' She stopped and took a deep breath. 'I can't believe it. I can't. Look, I'm sure we're jumping to conclusions here. We've both – just got an idea in our heads and we're probably getting it all wrong. But – well, OK, I'll go and have a look. It's almost time for class anyway, and I've got to fetch my other shoes.'

Together they went down to the changing rooms,

where the word 'Paris' popped in and out of an excited buzz wafting through the doors. Inside, intense discussions about who would go and who wouldn't, and who would do what and how well, were going on in a welter of flared nostrils, lifted eyebrows and pursed lips. With an exasperated upward roll of her eyes towards Gareth, Harriet pushed in through the door. Marianne was at the centre of a bunch of girls all talking at the tops of their voices whilst shoving pins in their hair, easing shoes over their heels and tightening waist elastics even further with furtive glances into the mirrors.

'But you're *bound* to go, Marianne. He *loved* you.'

'And you're French. They'll have to send you – just think . . . they've trained the best French dancer since Guillaume here in England. They'll want to show you off, of course they will.'

'Best French dancer . . . huh,' came a caustic voice from the corner. 'The others must be rubbish, then.' The voice dripped contempt. Harriet quickly grabbed Marianne's arm as she whirled round towards Jessica. Jessica carried on doing her hair, smug and complacent, apparently looking at herself in the mirror but in reality sneaking a look at Marianne's furious face behind her in the glass.

'Sticks and stones,' muttered Harriet, trying to pull

Marianne away. The other girls stood back, some looking anxious but most grinning, ready to enjoy a real slanging match or, even better, a brawl. 'Come on, Marianne, leave it. You know what she's doing.'

'But she say French dancers are rubbish . . .' Marianne was almost spitting with fury.

This was no moment to try to mend the entente cordiale. Harriet made do with another 'never mind, just leave it,' and managed to drag Marianne away to the studio, forgetting to pick up her own shoes on the way. The resulting harsh words from the teacher turned Harriet's cheeks scarlet, but the disappointed faces of the girls cheated of their fight made the telling-off almost worth it.

After class there was still no list of names for the chosen few going to Paris. In her head, Harriet knew she wouldn't be going. 'Not good enough for the Company, not good enough for Paris,' she kept saying to herself, but surely, said her heart, there was just a chance. She knew she could dance the Little Swans; she was quick and she was the right height, short and, she knew, not fat, but just not skinny enough. But grey-haired Miss Esbester, who taught repertoire, was one of the few staff who really liked her work.

Miss Esbester liked girls who could jump, she said,

and Harriet could jump. Once she was warmed up, she could jump as high as the boys. She never quite understood how it happened but she did understand the feeling of hanging up there in the air for a second before deciding to come down. She had read that that was how Nijinsky, one of the greatest male dancers the world had ever known, had described it long ago, and she knew exactly what he meant.

Boys and girls were mostly taught separately, but Miss Esbester had once come into the studio when Harriet was mucking about with Gareth, keeping up with him step for step in a boy's solo he was learning. Miss Esbester had watched, her eyes getting wider and wider, as Harriet soared through the air across the wide studio space at Gareth's side. After that, sometimes she let Harriet dance a boy's part and Harriet felt herself come alive and fly. Harriet had a feeling Miss Esbester just might have put in a word for her before the assessments; but if she had, it hadn't been enough to persuade the Director then, so it probably wouldn't be now.

Two interminable days passed before the list went up – and in the strain of waiting, Harriet forgot about Marianne's sudden running away from the library. Marianne hadn't mentioned it and seemed quite normal, excited about the Paris trip like everyone else and showing off a new baggy sweatshirt and wool-ups she had bought at the Dance Shop that must have cost a bomb. Her father had paid for them.

'You know what 'e said?' said Marianne. ' 'e said "Marianne, if you're going to be a star, you must look like one",' and she rolled her eyes and laughed.

Harriet laughed too. 'He spoils you, your dad,' she said without rancour. Her own father spoilt her too, when he could. But Marianne's father drove a big, shiny Mercedes and hers a battered Ford. Marianne always had pointe shoes by the dozen and sometimes took a taxi home if they were out late. Harriet hardened her shoes with shellac and always got a bus to her digs in Bethnal Green. That was the difference between them and it didn't seem to matter.

Perhaps the reason it didn't matter was because when it came to mothers it was a different story. Harriet had wondered sometimes why Marianne, who lived with her father in a smart flat in Chelsea, so seldom went back to stay with her mother in Paris. It certainly wasn't that they couldn't afford it. And once, when her father had had to go away, she had chosen to come to Sheffield to stay with Harriet for the holidays instead of going to Paris. When they left, Marianne had hugged Harriet's mother hard and almost seemed not to want to leave. She rarely spoke about her own mother and Harriet had given up asking about her. All she ever got was a quick 'yes' or 'no' and a change of subject.

When the moment came and the lists went up, Harriet sat on a bench in the cloakroom, listening to the excited cries out in the hall, miserably hugging her knees, as if hugging a last wisp of hope that she might, just might, be going to Paris. Other despondent girls began to trickle in, banging down bags in fury or simply in tears.

With a deep breath, Harriet went up to the hall and quickly ran her eye down the list. There was Marianne with Gareth for the new pas de deux. Jessica and Will were understudies, not Peter. Harriet spared a moment of sympathy for him, then carried on down the names. She needed no more than a cursory glance before she shrugged and turned away. Her name wasn't there. She had known it wouldn't be, of course she had, but still . . .

As she walked away from the board she met Marianne.

' 'Arry,' said Marianne, ' 'Arry, I'm so sorry . . .'

Harriet swallowed and lifted her chin. 'Didn't really think I'd be going, did you?'

'I think . . . I thought you would do the Little Swans.'

'Nope. Not a hope.' Harriet tried braving a wobbly grin. 'I'd have been the biggest Little Swan ever. All those French, they'd all have laughed and pointed. Couldn't have that.'

'But not even an understudy . . .'

'Not even an understudy. But listen, Marianne, I'm really, really glad you and Gareth are doing the pas de deux,' she said, and she meant it. Marianne plumped down on one of the high-backed chairs in the hall with a face so woebegone that Harriet almost laughed.

'I don't want to go without you,' said Marianne.

'Rubbish,' said Harriet, 'of course you do. Listen, you're going to dance a lead with Gareth, get to see your mum in Paris, what more do you want?'

'You to be there too,' said Marianne.

'Well, I won't be,' said Harriet brusquely, tears threatening suddenly, 'so there it is. Can't be helped.' There was a silence as she took a breath, blinked hard and tried changing the subject to stop the tears from gathering. 'Will you stay with your mum, d'you think? You haven't seen her for ages, have you?'

'Non,' said Marianne, 'we all have to stay together. A hostel, they said, but I'm not sure where yet. I will see my mother of course, but—' Before she could say any more, Will came prancing up the passageway, tra-lahing away at the *Marseillaise* at the top of his voice, with Gareth trying to look serious beside him. When Gareth saw Harriet, he gave Will a quick nudge and he stopped.

'It's all right,' said Harriet. 'I know, Marianne knows, we all know. I'm not going to Paris.' She managed another wobbly grin. 'Just as well, my French is awful.'

Will gave her shoulder a quick squeeze that nearly set her off properly. She ducked her head, swallowed and tried again.

'Marianne, will you be—?' But Marianne had vanished. Harriet looked round. 'Where did she go this time?'

Gareth shrugged and shook his head. He jerked a thumb towards the front doors. 'That-a-way,' he said. He turned to the notice-board and they started to discuss the programme and the casting.

Suddenly, the doors burst open and Marianne flew in, her mobile in her hand.

'You can come, 'Arry,' she said. 'You can come too.'

'What do you mean?'

'I speak to my father.'

'And?' said Gareth.

' 'E want – wants you to go too, with me, so I 'ave company.'

'But – but what will *they* say?' said Harriet, jerking her head towards the staff offices upstairs.

'My father will talk to them and to my mother.'

'What's your mum got to do with it?'

Marianne sat on the stairs, dragging Harriet after her. Gareth and Will gathered round.

'My father knows what it is like 'ere,' she said. ' 'E knows that Jessica and 'er friends are not my friends and that she might be . . . well, you know 'ow she can be to me.'

Harriet knew.

' 'E want me to 'ave you with me. He will call the Director and make it OK. You can stay with my mother and—'

Harriet's eyes widened. 'Marianne – I – I don't know your mother . . . I mean . . . Will you be there?'

Marianne shook her head quickly. 'Non, non. Like I say, I must stay with – with the company.' She nodded with a quick, proud little smile. 'But you can be with us all the time, except to go 'ome to sleep. My mother, she live very close to the Opéra, near the Grands Boulevards. You will love it.'

Harriet wasn't so sure. Something in her longed to go . . . but it wasn't the same to go not really belonging with the others, just a hanger-on . . . And then there was Marianne's mother, well . . . why would Marianne never talk about her?

'But supposing *they* don't want me to come?'

'My father will fix, you'll see.' Marianne smiled happily with the air of someone who is rarely disappointed.

Gareth flung an arm round Harriet. 'Harry, that's great,' he said, giving her a hefty pat. 'Come on, you can't say no to an offer like that.'

'Well,' said Harriet. 'There's always *my* mum. What's she going to say? She doesn't even know I'm not cast, yet.'

The sudden thought of telling her mother almost overwhelmed her. She'd understand, of course she would. She had been upset about the assessments but not angry, just indignant, certain her Harriet was as good a dancer as any of them. But going to Paris like this? Staying with someone she didn't know? Would she be all right in Paris on her own? Why did she have to go at all if she wasn't dancing? All that stuff. But she would let her go, Harriet was sure, because she and her dad always believed in her ability to make decisions and do what was right.

'Oh, come on! She'll want you to go, won't she? Mine would – bless!' said Will.

'There's money,' said Harriet.

'My father—' said Marianne.

'No,' said Harriet. 'Enough's enough. If I go, I pay my own way. If there isn't room for me on the bus, then—'

'I'll shove you in my ballet bag and zip it up for good, if you don't shut up,' said Will, hands on hips, tapping one foot dramatically. 'Go and phone your mum right now.'

Harriet hesitated.

'Go *on*!'

Pursing her lips and shaking her head, Harriet went.

# Chapter 4

Rehearsals with Alistair for the pas de deux went well. He didn't seem to mind one or two onlookers and there were usually several in the studio watching quietly. Harriet quite often managed to squeeze in behind the piano, sitting on her bottom with her knees up to her chin, making herself small and invisible while she watched every movement, dancing them in her head with Marianne.

Alistair's work was difficult but beautiful, full of strange, convoluted lifts. The counting too, seemed bizarre, but once Marianne and Gareth became familiar with the hand positions needed for each lift, swifter and more accurate with every repetition, the rhythm seemed to flow and the meaning of the dance became clear.

Alistair never gave any hint as to a story or a theme even, but to Harriet it seemed to be about the growing and blooming of a flower, with Gareth the strong stem and Marianne the delicate blossom tossed by wind and rain, and finally the petals opening to meet the sun's rays before the flower faded. Marianne seemed weightless, her long, slender legs stretching endlessly from position to position as Gareth supported her, protected her, sustained her, making it all seem easy even though it was the most challenging piece Harriet had ever seen any of the students attempt.

Not so for Jessica and Will. To be sure, Will had his flighty ways, but in spite of all that he was a strong partner. But Jessica was querulous, constantly finding fault with the way he partnered her. Whatever went wrong, everything was his fault. If she missed a leap, he had dropped her; if she missed a pirouette, he had pushed her off balance. She constantly fussed around, placing his hands 'just so' the way she wanted them, regardless of what Will or even Alistair was saying. Harriet wondered why they didn't just give up on her, but Will's flip sense of humour always came to the rescue. Harriet knew this really got to Jessica, but made it impossible for her to carry on being difficult without being thrown out altogether.

A few days before they were due to leave for Paris, Alistair gave both pairs an individual run-through in costume. Harriet, crouching in her corner behind the piano, regarded the boys' simple grey tights and tight V-necked T-shirts with no sleeves. They looked like two shadows as they warmed up in front of the mirrors, Gareth tall and elegant, Will shorter but strong and muscular, spiky curls highlighted now with a restrained blond, pulled back under a tight hair-band. The girls had silver-grey all-in-ones with a soft, silky calf-length skirt that drifted and billowed as they ran and leapt, spinning swiftly under their partner's arm or floating above their heads practising the lifts before tackling the pas de deux proper.

Gareth and Marianne went first. The strange music started slowly and gathered speed as they launched into the dance. Harriet gave a little shiver. In the costumes, it was less like watching a flower grow, more like watching water ripple peacefully, then faster and faster, bubbling and sparkling towards waves that tumbled into a crescendo as the last lift reached its highest peak and Gareth ran the length of the studio with Marianne above him, soaring like a grey bird over the sea.

Suddenly there was a sharp sound. Someone sneezed loudly. Harriet whipped her head round, appalled. What an awful thing to do – sneezing like that in the middle of a rehearsal! When she looked back, Marianne was falling. Gareth held her and slid her to the floor but her skirt caught between his legs and he stumbled, dropping forward, taking his weight on his arms to avoid crushing her beneath him. The music jangled to a stop and there was a breathless silence. Then Gareth rolled away from Marianne and huddled on the floor, clutching his shoulder and groaning. Harriet leapt to her feet. Alistair and Miss McGregor ran forward. Marianne scrambled to her knees and shuffled over to Gareth. His eyes were shut and he grunted in pain.

'Dislocated,' said Miss McGregor, shortly. 'Harriet, get his sweatshirt, something, anything. We must keep him warm. Marianne, put something on, quickly, you mustn't get cold either.'

Will flung a top to Harriet. Miss McGregor took it and wrapped it gently round Gareth's shoulders. Harriet grimaced and drew in a breath as she saw the ugly bulge where the bone had slipped out of place. Gareth sat up slowly, his face creased up, one arm wrapped round himself, tenderly probing the injury with his fingers. Marianne knelt beside him, shaking a little.

'Garette, oh, Garette, I'm so sorry...'

'It's not your fault,' he said with a weak grin. 'I must have lost my concentration when that noise came. Someone sneezed or something ...

Look, are you all right? You're not hurt?'

Marianne shook her head. 'I'm OK,' she said. 'It was a shock coming down like that, but I – I'm OK.' She looked away for an instant, dropping her head. Quietly, Miss McGregor put her sweatshirt over her head and she almost automatically pulled it on and hugged it to her.

'Oh, Marianne, I'm so, so sorry. I just—' said Gareth.

'Look,' said Alistair, 'it doesn't matter now. You've got to get to hospital and, well . . . I'm sorry, Gareth, but I'm going to have to get on and rehearse Marianne with Will. There's no way you can dance the pas de deux now.'

'They'll put my shoulder back, won't they? It'll be all right?'

Miss McGregor shook her head. 'No, Gareth. They will put the shoulder back, of course, but it means a while before you can dance. The muscles will be in spasm and you'll probably need physio. I'm afraid it means no Paris for you.'

Gareth's shoulders drooped. He flinched and hastily pulled himself upright. He looked down at Marianne.

'I'm so – so sorry . . .' he said again.

She put her hands to her mouth and burst into

tears. 'It wasn't – I – I don't want to – I can't . . . Oh, Garette . . .'

'Yes you do, you can,' whispered Harriet. She squatted down beside her but Marianne was sobbing, twisting her fingers, pushing her hands into her thighs. As Harriet put an arm round her, she noticed the little round bones sticking out at the back of her neck like tiny white pebbles. She frowned; but now was not the moment to say anything. Beside them, Alistair and Will were helping Gareth to struggle into a chair. As she looked up, Harriet noticed Jessica standing by the barre, her face like thunder. She quickly turned away from Harriet's eyes and started nonchalantly stretching.

*It was you.* The thought flashed through Harriet's mind. *You sneezed. You wanted it to be Marianne that got hurt, not Gareth . . . You – you . . .* But she said nothing. There was no proof, and anyway, Gareth had to be got to hospital and the pas de deux started almost from the beginning. But she was sure she was right. Jessica had disrupted the rehearsal deliberately. Her arm tightened round Marianne's shoulder.

'Marianne, it's OK. You'll be fine with Will, won't she, Will?' Gareth managed to sound reassuring, but his face was pale and he still clutched his shoulder.

Will nodded. ' 'Course you will,' he said with a

confident grin, holding out his hand to Marianne, but he glanced at Harriet standing behind her, and almost imperceptibly flickered his eyes wide.

'Come on, La Mari*ah*na. Don't get stressed. You've got Will the Boy Wonder at your side. Best crane in the business – well, second best.' He nodded his blond highlights at Gareth. Marianne dropped her head, about to cry, and he squatted beside her, suddenly serious.

'Come on, Marianne. Let's just have a go and see what happens, hm? I know I'm not Gareth, but . . .' He sprang up and did a 'Mr Atlas', flexing his muscles and posing.

'Always you joke,' said Marianne through her tears, but she let Will pull her up from her knees. She straightened her skirt and wiped her hand across her nose and her eyes. Harriet let out a quiet 'pffff' of relief and gave Will a grateful grin. With a deep shuddering breath, Marianne looked from Will to Alistair and gave a little nod.

'Good girl,' said Alistair and gave her a hug. 'Come on, let's see what you can do, the two of you.'

'Now? Can't we do it tomorrow? I – I . . .'

'Marianne, you aren't hurt, are you? Just a bit shaken.'

She nodded reluctantly.

'Then it's best to do it straight away. Like getting on a horse when you've fallen off. You'll have to warm up again, carefully. Come on . . .'

Marianne looked at Gareth, her face still troubled, but he nodded.

'Go on,' he said, 'do it for both of us, OK?'

Will put a hand on her arm and Marianne allowed herself to be led back to the centre of the studio. Miss McGregor took the costume skirt from her and draped it over the barre. Marianne pulled on some wool-ups over the grey all-in-one, slipping the straps under her sweatshirt. She added a waist elastic, giving it an extra knot to tighten it even more. She smoothed down her hair and pushed down her toes into her pointe shoes. Alistair took her hand and gently started to mark through the first pirouette with her.

Harriet glanced across at Jessica, who had stayed by the barre, still stretching her feet and legs, with apparently no more than one eye on proceedings. Her face was bland now but there was a faint twitch in her lips that told Harriet she was still angry. Angry that it was Gareth who was injured and not Marianne, no doubt. Well, hard luck.

Miss McGregor helped Gareth away from the studio, his track-suit top dangling round his shoulders, held tightly by his good hand. Harriet carried his bag and waited with him in the hall. Miss McGregor asked a passing student to fetch his clothes from the cloakroom and sent for a male teacher to go with him in the ambulance. Harriet wanted to go, but Miss McGregor said it had to be a member of staff.

As the ambulance drove away, Harriet looked at Miss McGregor. 'Umm. Miss McGregor . . . Who was it that sneezed?' she asked.

'I don't know. Whoever it was should be—' She broke off quickly. 'I don't suppose we'll ever find out. Well, it's done now.' She shook her head impatiently and headed up to the offices to phone Gareth's parents. Harriet watched her go. No one had apologized. No one had seemed guilty or embarrassed. It had been a very loud sneeze and dancers knew better than to interrupt a rehearsal like that. A sneeze could have been, should have been muffled. It had to have been Jessica.

She crept back into the rehearsal. Jessica was sitting out looking mutinous, without a partner. It was too late for Peter to learn the pas de deux now. There were too many rehearsals for too many other things to fit in before they left. Jessica made no move to mark the part but glared at Marianne through each step. *The evil eye*, thought Harriet as she slipped behind the piano. *Well, lousy Jessica. You can't even rehearse the pas de deux now. There won't be time for you to have more than a couple of goes with Will if you're lucky and that'll be about it. And serve you right.* And she slid her back down the wall and plumped softly on to her bottom, dropping her knees out sideways into a frog and leaning on them with her elbows.

Alistair was taking it slowly, analysing each move and patiently reworking the basics of the lifts and turns that Will's height made necessary. Serious for once, Will talked to Marianne about each step thoughtfully and sensitively, and within an hour they began to put the dance together.

Jessica looked like thunder as the rehearsal ended and the studio cleared.

'How's your cold?' said Harriet quietly as she passed her on her way out. Jessica stiffened but walked on. Then she swung round.

'What do you mean?' she said. 'Are you trying to—?'

Harriet looked her squarely in the eye. Jessica flushed and tossed her head.

'Oh, you're not worth bothering with,' she said and stalked off.

'Hmm,' said Harriet to herself. 'I can't prove anything and you know it. What you did was terrible, really terrible, but at least you didn't get your way, madam lousy Jessica, and maybe you've even learnt a lesson.'

She turned. Alistair was still talking to Marianne and Will, an arm round each of their shoulders. Will was nodding, his face wreathed in his usual grin. He bent forward and looked Marianne straight in the eyes till she managed a smile. Alistair patted her arm and went over to the pianist. Marianne hurried towards Harriet.

'Ça va? It was all right?'

' 'Course it was,' said Harriet. 'It's going to be really good.'

'It's not the same.'

'Maybe not, but Will's great, Marianne. He's really giving it all he's got.'

'I know, I know.' She pulled on another sweater. 'But I feel so shaky and—'

'Listen, you've had a shock. It was awful what happened back there. 'Course you're shaky. But you got up and got on with it, like I knew you would. You'll feel better tomorrow. And I bet they'll want you to do the pas de deux with Gareth at the end of year show. He'll be better by then.'

Marianne nodded miserably. 'Poor Garette.' She gave a shiver.

'Come on. What you need now is some food.'

But Marianne shook her head. 'Just some tea,' she said. 'I'm too tired to eat now. I'll eat later.'

Harriet's spirits fell and she thought of the bones in Marianne's neck. And there was no Gareth to share the worries with now. She followed Marianne from the studio and took her arm, steering her firmly towards the canteen in case she changed her mind.

'OK, then,' she said, 'but hot chocolate at least. You need the energy.'

But Marianne would only take peppermint tea and refused even a biscuit. Harriet didn't dare insist. She felt that Marianne was still very close to tears and that she'd had enough for one day. Going on about food would be pushing her too far.

'Later. I will eat later, chez moi,' said Marianne. 'The food here is . . .' and she wrinkled her nose. She sipped her tea but gave up and pushed it away. She picked up her bag and bent to kiss Harriet's cheek. 'The pas de deux,' she said anxiously, 'it will be all right? Will is—'

'It'll be brilliant,' said Harriet and meant it.

Marianne smiled a crooked little smile. 'I will call Garette later to see how he is,' she said, 'just in case.'

'Marianne, I wouldn't get your hopes up . . .'

'No, but . . .' She shrugged and walked away, hugging her bag close in front of her like a shield. Harriet shook her head. She would phone Gareth later too, of course, but she knew that he wouldn't be dancing in Paris. With a sigh, she gathered her things and went up to the library to sort out which books she wanted to take with her on the trip. She wouldn't be allowed to do anything more than watch class if she was lucky, certainly not join in, so she would need something to keep her mind occupied.

In the cool of the coming evening, the deserted library was shadowy and still. Harriet put on a single light, took down her books and looked through them. She thought she would take an English set book and the book with the photographs she had looked at with Marianne. In Paris there would be time to find out more about Giuseppina Bozzacchi, even go and see the places where she had lived, done class, and where the old Opéra had been. The librarian had even told her how to go about using the archive at the Opéra de Paris, if she felt venturesome. She slipped the set book into a pocket and then, with a little thrill of excitement, carefully put the book of photographs into her bag. She might not be going to dance, but still, Paris for the first time . . .

She turned out the light and opened the door. She paused. What was that? Behind her, someone was crying very softly. Harriet let the door close quietly and turned back. Perhaps Marianne had come up here instead of going straight home, or perhaps someone else was feeling low ... She looked around. The desks were empty and there was no movement anywhere. She walked back into the room, put down her bag and waited. Silence. She must have been mistaken. Just to be sure, she glanced along between the two or three rows of shelves that projected into the room, but there was no one there and she shook her head. She must have been hearing things after all the stress and strain of the afternoon. She gave herself a shake and bent to retrieve her bag.

As she straightened up, there was a sigh. She shivered uneasily. Who was here? Where were they? The sigh had sounded really close. The door behind her opened and the librarian looked in.

'Still here, Harriet? Time you went home.'

'Oh ... oh yes, yes. I just came for the books I'm taking to Paris.'

'Lucky girl. Have a good time.'

'Yes, yes, thank you. I will ... Er, Mrs Lewis, was there anyone in the passage as you came up?'

'No, no one. I've just come to lock up. Come on, off with you.'

Harriet opened the door. As she took its weight and it parted from its pair, it gave a sort of sigh. Of course, that's what it must have been. The door must have made that sound when she'd opened it before and then again as the librarian started to come in. She gave a little laugh, said goodnight and left.

But coming down the stairs she frowned. The sigh might be explained, but what about the crying? That had been real and it had sounded close . . . in the room, definitely not outside. She thought back. It had happened just after she'd put the book of photographs in her bag . . .

In the hall, she unzipped her bag and peered in, but the book lay inert and harmless. How stupid could you get? Just the same, she took it out and riffled through the pages till she found the photograph. Giuseppina Bozzacchi still knelt in her white tulle, her eyes downcast, her white hands still crossed at the wrist on her lap. She faced to the right, just as she had the first time. Or was it? Left, right? She couldn't remember . . . And the leaves down the front of her skirts . . . is that how they were? Hadn't they been falling down to one side a little, not straight over her knee like that?

She shut the book quickly. This really was stupid. She was letting her imagination run away with her now. But it had been a pretty terrible afternoon. The stress must be getting to her. She gave a big, pull-yourself-together sniff, replaced the book and stood up. Familiar sounds were all around: pianos competing with each other from the studios, laughter from a schoolroom, and through the front doors the sound of a bus swishing past with a quick blast on its horn. Up in the offices, a phone rang. Everything was normal.

*Get a grip, Harriet*, she thought, *get a grip, for goodness sake*. She slung the bag over her shoulder and stumped out.

# Chapter 5

'Listen, Harry, you will take care of her, won't you? She's – she's so – fragile . . .'

Even on the phone, Harriet could hear the lump in Gareth's throat.

'I know. But she'll be all right, Gareth. Don't worry. She and Will did fine once they'd got going. Will was brilliant . . . none of his funny stuff – you know – just really concentrating and making it work. And Alistair was right to make her go straight in. Best thing, honest.'

'Not just that,' he said. 'I mean – Harry, I really don't want to say this but – I – I think she fell because . . .'

'Because why?'

'Well . . .' She heard him take a deep breath. 'It wasn't *me* that dropped *her*, Harry. She couldn't keep the hold in the lift when whoever it was sneezed. She was startled, I know, we both were, but it was Marianne that lost the hold, not me.'

'Might have happened to anyone, mightn't it? It was pretty loud.'

'Yes, but . . . It wasn't so much the shock. She just wasn't strong enough to hold it. She's weaker than she was, Harry. I could tell. And she's wearing all those baggy sweatshirts and stuff, wool-ups and track-suit bottoms all the time like – like a suit of armour. Alistair practically had to tear them off her the other day so he could see what she was doing.'

'Well, it's easy to get cold in rehearsals. Easier than in class if you have to wait about while things get worked out.'

'Fat chance with Alistair. He works you hard – you don't stop. And – and yesterday I thought she was going to give at the knees, she was so weak.'

'Why didn't you say?'

'It was at the end when we'd been going a long time, so I told myself she was just over-the-top tired. And I guess I didn't want it to be true, either. Like you said.'

Harriet nodded glumly into the phone.

'Harry, I wasn't sure. The pas de deux's difficult, it wipes you out . . . And then today, with more people there . . . Miss McGregor, everyone . . .'

'Don't tell me – in public, the boy takes the blame.

But, Gareth, it's *not* always the boy's fault when something goes wrong. I know it's what we *say*, but . . .'

'No, but – oh, Harry, as soon as it happened, I knew I wouldn't be dancing in Paris. I didn't want to mess it up for Marianne too by saying she'd – she'd collapsed . . .'

'Come on, Gareth, you'd never have said that, anyway.'

'I guess not. Look – it's not long now, she's surely strong enough to last till then and afterwards we'll do something about it. She should dance the pas de deux, Harry, she's done all the work and she's the best. Jessica sucks in it. You know she does.'

'True. She hasn't got the feel of it at all.' She paused. 'Gareth . . . Listen . . . I think – I'm pretty sure it was Jessica that sneezed.'

'*What?*'

'No one's saying they did it, of course, and no one seems to be asking. Maybe *they* just don't want problems when we're so close to the performance. If they knew, whoever it was would be in real trouble. Maybe even chucked out of the performance and they don't want that *now*. I haven't got proof, of course, but that's who I think it was. Lousy Jessica.'

'Oh jeez. And I'm not going to be there if she has

another go. What a mess. Harriet—'

'She's not likely to risk anything really major like that again. It'll just be needle, needle, needle at Marianne. But Will and I can keep an eye out for her. I'll talk to him. But what about Marianne and the – the eating business? D'you really think she's that weak? She doesn't show any signs in class – at least . . . I don't think so.' Only yesterday there had been the odd stumble, but nothing serious, surely . . . just a tricky step . . .

Gareth broke in. 'No, don't mention that to Will. The fewer people who know about it the better, for now. A week and this'll all be over. Just let her do the pas de deux without too much fuss and then we'll talk to someone. Just make sure you or Will are with her as much as you can and keep lousy Jessica away from her.'

Harriet sighed. How was she really supposed to do that if she wasn't staying in the hostel with Marianne?

'We'll do what we can between us,' she said. 'Somehow . . . Anyway, how are you?'

'Well – my shoulder's not so bad. It's back in place but it aches like hell and I get nasty twinges. Got to rest it and can't dance probably for a month.'

'Oh, Gareth!'

'Never mind. It's not terminal.' He gave a rueful laugh. 'I might even get my project done now – I *don't* think.' Gareth danced like a dream but he wasn't the world's best academic student.

'I'm sorry, I'm sorry, I'm sorry. What a mess!'

'Oh well, what's done . . . Jeez, why did it have to happen? Lousy Jessica! I just *wish* I was there. I feel so helpless sitting here doing nothing. Listen, take care of her. Do your best, Harry, please . . . Keep in touch.'

Obviously upset, Gareth rang off quickly. Harriet pushed her way out of the phone booth in the hall. Keeping in touch wouldn't be so easy. Phoning from a phone booth in Paris would cost a bomb and she had no mobile. But talking to Gareth now, Harriet realized how vital it was that she did go to Paris. Will might be around to help take care of any trouble from Jessica, but Marianne was much weaker than she, Harriet, had realized.

Well . . . she'd just have to hope that Marianne got through the performance without any more traumas. And Marianne wanted her to go so badly, that in spite of her worry, the thought made Harriet smile. She just wished she could go for the fun and the excitement of being with Marianne in Paris without this other horrible business, secret and scary, starting to come between them.

In the hall, she heard crying. Real crying this time. Harriet turned down the corridor to the studios. Marianne was sitting in a huddled heap on a bench against the wall. Harriet dumped her bag and dropped to her knees in front of her. She reached up, took Marianne's hands and pulled them gently away from her face. Her heart dropped as she saw the gaunt hollows round Marianne's eyes. Close to like this, her cheekbones stuck out under the skin like the bleached white razor-shells you sometimes found on the beach in summer.

'What is it? What's wrong?' she managed to say, forcing herself to look into Marianne's eyes and not stare at her face. Marianne just shook her head and looked away down the corridor.

'Are you hurt? Marianne! Answer me!'

Marianne shook her head again and slid her knees down, preparing to get up. Harriet shifted out of the way but caught Marianne's hand.

'Marianne, tell me. What's happened? Is it Gareth? Will?'

Marianne simply went on shaking her head, smearing her face with her hand and edging up the bench away from Harriet.

Harriet jumped to her feet. 'Marianne. Please tell me what's wrong. I can't help if you don't tell me.'

Marianne sat very still for a moment and then glanced up at Harriet, her brow furrowed and her mouth trembling. She pressed her hands against her hips, pushed them down over her thighs, digging in hard, looking down.

'I – I – it's nothing. 'Arry, leave me alone. I'm OK.'

'Oh yeah? You look fine, just fine. Marianne, come on. Let's get this sorted. You can't go on like this. You're going to get ill.'

Marianne jumped up, angry now. 'I'm not ill, I'm not. There's nothing wrong with me. Nothing wrong except . . .'

Harriet said nothing but looked a question. Marianne slumped back on to the bench, her anger dissolving into misery. Harriet held her breath. Maybe Marianne would spill now. Harriet knew that the worst part of – of what she thought might be wrong with Marianne was getting whoever it was to admit there was a problem.

Marianne stopped crying. Her face was still pink from anger and she didn't look quite so bad. Harriet found herself hoping, telling herself that she and Gareth must be wrong after all.

She sat beside Marianne and put an arm round her shoulder. Marianne was wearing a thick woollen sweater. What would she feel like underneath it?

Harriet couldn't tell. But Marianne turned her head into Harriet's own soft, rounded shoulder and started to cry again quietly, calmer this time, as if the storm was over. Suddenly Harriet knew.

'It's Jessica, isn't it?' she said, not knowing whether to be relieved not to have to confront the other problem after all. 'Lousy, lousy Jessica . . . She's full of – full of – tschhh . . .' She leant back against the wall, casting her eyes at the ceiling and grasping the edge of the bench, hunching her shoulders. Then she swung round to Marianne.

'She's rubbish, Marianne. She'll say anything to upset you so she can do the pas de deux instead of you. That's what this is all about. Can't you see?'

Marianne looked at her with big eyes and gave a little nod. Harriet paused. Marianne looked at her still, hugging her big woolly round her. Harriet gave a little grin.

'Anyway,' she said, 'what *did* she say?'

Marianne managed a little grin back.

'Stuff,' she said, 'you know.'

'Whatever it was, it's all – all – garbage.'

'She say – said Gareth drop me because I am so 'eavy.' Harriet let out a hoot. 'She said Will wouldn't be able to manage because of my – my weight. She said the pas de deux would be a – a désastre – a disaster.'

'Come on, Marianne – you don't believe that for a minute. Jessica weighs a tonne more than you. And anyway you've already got it together with Will. Alistair's pleased. And Jessica saw you. Just don't let her wind you up. Listen, have you spoken to Gareth since he got 'ome from the hospital?'

Marianne shook her head. 'I will call him tonight when I get 'ome,' she said. ' 'Ave you?'

Harriet nodded. 'They've put his shoulder back. It still hurts, aches and twinges. He won't be able to dance for a while, but we knew that. He'll tell you himself when you call him. And what about Will? What did he say after the rehearsal?'

'Oh, you know Will,' said Marianne, smiling at last, ''e turn a pirouette – eight turns – wiggle about a bit and smile with big teeth.'

'Says it all,' said Harriet with a laugh. 'But he was great in rehearsal.'

'Yes, 'e was. 'E was. So good. Not Garette but – very good.'

'No one's like "Garette",' said Harriet with a little sideways nod, 'but Will's OK. He's – he's *OK*.' And she nodded some more, energetically, looking under her eyebrows at Marianne.

Marianne was looking better. Harriet picked up both their bags, slung them over her shoulder and dragged her up by the hand.

'You should go home and eat, Marianne. And then phone Gareth. And *then* get some sleep. It's not long now.'

They went out through the big double doors on to the street. Traffic was roaring by on the dual carriageway out of the city, riffling the bright new leaves of the big plane tree outside. Tall buildings towered on either side of the school, dwarfing it, the glass in their windows seeming to rattle with vibration from the passing cars and lorries, an occasional helmeted cyclist zipping along the bus lane like a knight errant on a quest. Litter and dust blew in spurts along the gutter, a Coke can rolling and rattling as it went.

'You want me to come with you on the bus?' Harriet shouted against the din.

Marianne shook her head, her face wrinkled up against the fumes. 'I think I will get a taxi,' she said.

'Good idea,' yelled Harriet, 'after all that. You want me to come home with you?'

Marianne thought for a moment and then said, 'Non, non, I'm all right now, 'Arry. And my dad is there with 'is new girlfriend. They may have plans.'

'And you've got to phone Gareth. You'll be hours talking to him, I bet.'

Harriet didn't push it. To be honest, she was relieved. She would rather be alone with her thoughts right now. And she wasn't comfortable in Marianne's posh flat with her dad speaking French to Marianne and then breaking into English just for her, so that she always felt only half there. And the girlfriend would mean extra stress. 'I need to do some sorting out before we go,' she said. 'I'll see you first thing tomorrow.'

Marianne hailed a cab and scrambled in. It nosed into the traffic, cocooning her against the noise outside, and sailed off. Harriet stood at the kerb in the haze and dust and waved at Marianne peering through the back window of the taxi as it rolled away. She turned and hurried off towards the bus stop, feeling a bit better. Marianne seemed calmer and more together, and in a week, as Gareth said, it would all be over. With a little surge of excitement, Harriet thought of Paris. But her face quickly clouded over. A lot could happen in a week, good and bad. This just wasn't how going to Paris for the first time was meant to be . . .

# Chapter 6

The coach swept round the Arc de Triomphe and headed down the Champs Élysées.

'Never been to Paris?' Marianne had said. 'You must sit next to the window and see *everything*.' So Harriet sat with her nose glued to the window, eyes like satellite saucers, fogging up the glass with her breath and wiping it off with her sleeve.

'I'm used to big cities,' she said. 'Sheffield and London and that. But this . . . this is something else, Marianne.' And Marianne beamed with proprietorial pride.

Harriet gasped at the expanse of the long avenue as it opened up before them, gently sloping down between graceful trees to a vast crossroads. In the distance, the road rose up again to a square where tiny cars buzzed like angry wasps round a stone obelisk on an island in the centre – the Place de la Concorde. Tall, slender buildings, old and dignified, stood back behind the trees. Discreetly decorated with plaster mouldings, their long, narrow windows twinkled as if they might be guarding naughty secrets in rooms high above gorgeous displays in the elegant, modern shop windows at street level.

Let into the pavement surrounding the base of each tree spaced out along the avenue was an intricate wrought-iron wheel protecting the trunk. Dark green wrought-iron kiosks flaunted cascades of multicoloured magazines like paper waterfalls. Flocks of brilliant umbrellas clustered inside the glass walls outside café after café, and crowds of people strolled along the broad pavements, or sat chatting, seeming to talk with their hands, chic, vivacious, yet appearing so unhurried . . .

'There's so much – so much *room*,' said Harriet, thinking about the narrow pavement of the roaring, traffic-choked road outside the school, where you had to shout to speak and sitting around was unthinkable. 'And it's so – so cheerful-looking, all the colours – like a kaleidoscope, changing all the time. London's soft and grey, Paris is kind of – kind of *silver* – sparkly silver. And you can practically taste the cafés – all those weird-looking fish on those stalls outside with the lemons and the ice packed all round them . . .'

'And the smells,' said Marianne, with a laugh, 'du vrai café enfin. Real good coffee everywhere, not like that canteen stuff you 'ave.'

Maybe that was it; maybe Marianne just missed French cooking. Maybe she did eat at home with her French father. Maybe she would eat now she was home. Harriet's hopes rose. Anyway, impossible to be worried or depressed in this magical place. She went on peering through the window as the sun came out and cast lacy, black shadows from the trees across the flagstones, and the tempo of the crowds slowed even further. The coach drove on down the avenue across the wide crossroads where an arcaded building, all wrought iron and glass, the front like the ribs of a huge open fan, glittered in the sun, brushed by the branches of the ancient trees crowded round it. Ahead was a park, but not like the rolling grass mounds of the London park near where she lived. Trees stood guard in regimented lines on either side of gravel walks set out in a geometric pattern, the acid green of their still-new leaves standing out against the deep emerald of the squares of grass between them.

As the coach revved and launched itself into the whirling traffic of the Place de la Concorde, towering over the trees Harriet saw a great palace, its side-wings stretching towards her like two arms. They held between them a stone arch, covered with carving. Through the arch she caught a glimpse of a big glass pyramid, glinting in the sun.

'The Louvre,' said Marianne, 'that's the Louvre. It was a royal palace. Grander than Buckingham Palace, non?'

'Grander than Buckingham Palace, oui,' said Harriet with a smile. 'Can we go there?'

'Maybe. If there's time. It's 'uge. You could stay there for days and not see it all.'

'I know,' said Harriet, 'and I have to admit, it's – it's well, it's more "chouette" than I'd imagined from pictures.' And Marianne laughed again at her meagre attempt at being French in France.

The coach swung away from the roar of the Place de la Concorde and the Louvre was gone. They drew up outside the hostel in a quiet street off a main road not far from the Opéra. The school had allowed Harriet to travel on the bus, but not to take Gareth's place in the hostel as he would have been sharing with Will. Will wouldn't have minded and nor would Harriet, but the school secretary thought differently. Harriet was still to stay with Marianne's mother.

As the door slid open, the students stood up and stretched, reached down their hand baggage and tumbled down the steps to scramble their bigger bags from the bowels of the coach. Harriet stood clutching her rucksack as Marianne looked about for Mme Dupont, her mother's housekeeper. She was to meet Harriet and make sure she knew the way from the apartment to the Opéra where, it had been agreed, Harriet could watch class and rehearsals.

Mme Dupont was short and stout, with fresh pink cheeks that made up for the beginnings of a moustache and stray whiskers on her chin. But her bright blue eyes smiled as she hugged Marianne tight and turned to kiss Harriet on both cheeks when they were introduced. Harriet stood back shyly as Marianne chattered away to the old lady in French, noticing her little frown as she hugged Marianne again then suddenly held her away from her, feeling down her shoulders and arms under their thick sweater with her chubby fingers.

'Tu as maigri, ma petite,' she said with a little wag of her head. Harriet recognized that word. 'You have got thin, little one.' 'Maigrir' was a word she had heard Marianne sometimes mutter to herself these days and she'd looked it up in the dictionary. But Marianne gave a little smile, shook her head and said something that included the words 'pas de deux' and 'travail' – 'work' – that seemed to satisfy Mme

Dupont for the moment at least. She turned to Harriet.

'Alors,' she said, and Harriet suddenly became anxious that she wouldn't be able to understand this woman, nice as she seemed. And what about Marianne's mother? She spoke English, she knew, but sometimes accents were difficult. Marianne hadn't told her very much at all, only her name really, Mademoiselle Mireille Cantal – and to be sure to use Mademoiselle not Madame . . .

'La petite 'Arriette,' said Mme Dupont. 'Zer littel 'Arriette. You come wit' me, oui? And I take care of you.'

Harriet's spirits quickly rose again. It would be quite nice to be taken care of by this comfortable person with the sparkle in her eye, especially as it looked as if she would understand her at least a bit. She looked at the dour, shabby-looking hostel, the students slowly disappearing inside, and gave Marianne a grin.

'I think I've got the best end of this,' she said. 'You sure you don't want to come too?'

Marianne smiled back but shook her head. 'No,' she said, 'the school say I must be with everyone else. And I think it is best like that.' She glanced away then looked at Harriet. 'I will – I will come to see

Maman perhaps tomorrow night after rehearsals, if she is – if she is free.'

Harriet frowned. *If she is free?* she thought. She couldn't imagine her own mother not being free if she was coming up to Sheffield for a couple of days. She'd probably be there to meet the bus, dragging Harriet's two brothers with her.

Mme Dupont tried to take her rucksack and Harriet wrestled with her, saying she would rather carry it herself. The old lady finally gave in and took her arm. Harriet turned back to Marianne standing on the pavement, all at once looking alone and vulnerable. Harriet hesitated. 'Will you be all right?'

'Leave her to me, duckie.' With a flutter of his fingers, Will appeared, dismissed Harriet and swept Marianne up the steps of the hostel, his enormous bag over his shoulder.

'Not unlike lumping our lousy Jessica around, stiff as a board and *almost* as heavy,' he mouthed quietly, jerking his head towards his bag. Harriet's eyes widened as Jessica passed and disappeared through the door behind him, but apparently she didn't hear. Will spun round and with a saucy flick of a foot almost kicking his bottom, he steered Marianne gently ahead of him into the dark hallway of the hostel.

Laughing, Harriet turned to Mme Dupont, who was laughing too.

'That's Will, Marianne's new partner,' said Harriet and then hesitated. Did Mme Dupont understand?

'Oui, oui,' she said. 'I understand. I understand more zan I can speak. But we will do very well, ma petite. Alors. Off we go, yes?'

'Off we go, yes,' said Harriet and heaved her rucksack on to her shoulder. She felt relieved. Will had obviously taken to heart the words of warning she'd managed to give him about Jessica and Marianne before they started. She could leave her now without so much worry.

They set off down the street beneath the tall grey buildings, the pavement narrower here and blotched with stains. Notices peeled off the walls; paint peeled from doors; fat cats plumped out over windowsills, their paws tucked beneath them, watching with lazy, suspicious eyes as they passed. Clear water trickled like a stream down the gutters and men in bright green jackets swept them with stiff brooms in the main street ahead of them.

'Zis Will,' said Mme Dupont as they went, ' 'e remind me of someone I know – knew a long time ago.' She threw Harriet a glance. She spoke slowly and carefully, but her eyes danced. ' 'E was my partenaire. Jackie, 'e was called. English. I was danseuse too, hein? Difficult to – er – to . . .'

'Believe?' said Harriet, without thinking. It was, indeed, very difficult to believe, looking at the dumpy figure trotting along beside her, a forest of kirbigrips sticking out of her tight little grey bun. She had been a dancer?

'Believe, yes. Zat is it. But, chérie, we don't forget, you know, it is still in zer – zer blood.' And to Harriet's astonishment, Mme Dupont grabbed her arm, took her skirt in her hand and kicked her little fat leg high in the air, level with her nose.

'See?' said Mme Dupont, puffing slightly. 'We don't forget.'

A group of workmen on scaffolding across the road gave a cheer and clanged their spanners against the metal.

'No,' said Harriet, laughing. She ought to be embarrassed but she wasn't. She was in Paris and anything could happen. Instead, she kicked her own jeans-clad leg up past her ear somewhere.

'No, we don't forget.'

There was another cheer and more clanging from the workmen, and she blushed and straightened her T-shirt, suddenly remembering herself. Paris must be getting under her skin.

'An' if we forget,' said Mme Dupont, 'zer legs do not,' and she cackled with laughter, throwing her head back, showing her yellowing teeth and shedding kirbigrips all over the flagstones.

'Bon, alors,' she said, hugging Harriet's arm, 'we shall be good friends, I t'ink,' and she hurried on, twinkling at everyone, left and right, till even the cats overflowing the windowsills seemed to grin back.

The apartment building was very grand. They had left the shabby part of the town near the hostel, crossed the Grand Boulevard and entered a courtyard through a tiny door let into huge double doors studded with metal. Inside, to the left, the top half of a door stood open. A thin, sour-looking concierge glanced out from the room inside. Mme Dupont gave her a chirpy 'Bonjour, Madame,' but the woman nodded stiffly. Mme Dupont went over and leant through the open door. Harriet heard her name mentioned and the woman stared out at her for a moment, nodded and turned away. She did not go so far as to slam the half-door shut, but her back made it clear the conversation was at an end.

Mme Dupont winked at Harriet. 'Qu'est-ce qu'elle est moche,' she said, in not too hushed a tone, 'dés-agré-able! Mais . . . do not worry, 'Arriet, she know who you are now. She make no trouble when you enter alone. Understand?' Harriet nodded and they crossed the shady courtyard where dozens of scarlet geraniums burst into bud in the window boxes on every side and on every floor, up and up, way above her head to the square of blue sky beyond.

At the top of a short, dark stair, another double-door let them into the apartment. Harriet looked round and shrank, suddenly feeling small and insignificant. She hugged her rucksack to her and swallowed hard. All she had was a change of jeans, a couple of T-shirts and a sweater, and her ballet things just in case *they* relented. If Miss Esbester was taking class, she just might . . .

But standing on the thick, fringed rug inside the doors, a polished floor stretching it seemed for miles on either side of her, she felt she should have brought, well . . . she had no really posh clothes, but at least a skirt or something . . . To make it worse there were mirrors everywhere. Wherever she turned she met herself, short and shabby and clutching her battered rucksack.

Mme Dupont saw her face. 'Oooh, là! Don't be sad, ma petite!' She pinched her cheek gently. 'Do not worry. You are – what is zer word – étudiante –

student. Not grand lady. You are fine. OK, hein? Mlle Cantal will not eat you, 'Arriette. And you can stay wit' me in zer kitchen most times. OK?'

Harriet gave a wan smile and nodded. Mme Dupont grabbed her rucksack and prodded her towards a door at the end of a short passage off the hallway where thankfully the mirrors ended. Inside was a tiny little room that looked over the courtyard but managed to catch the sun from over the rooftops and let in a cheery view of the geraniums of the apartments opposite. There was a little bed with a patchwork quilt, that seemed out of place against the heavy built-in cupboard and the smart chrome-handled chest-of-drawers. The bedside table also had a chrome-handled drawer and a modern-looking chrome lamp with a white shade. But in the corner a small white-painted bookcase bulged with ballet books.

The bed and the bookcase made Harriet feel a little better. It was as if at least a tiny part of Marianne was here. She realized that Mme Dupont was already unpacking her rucksack, shaking out her few things and hanging them in the cupboard. Harriet darted forward, but Mme Dupont simply plonked her down on the bed with one hand on her shoulder and went on hanging.

Suddenly at home, Harriet tucked her legs up out of the way and prepared for conversation.

'Was this – *is* this – Marianne's room?'

Mme Dupont nodded, still busy trying to get some sort of shape into Harriet's T-shirts. 'She live wit' 'er daddy – you say, daddy, yes? She live wit' 'er papa, alors, in Londres . . . London, while she study. It is sad. I miss 'er, la petite. I look after 'er when she was a baby, jus' born, but now . . .'

'She doesn't come home very often, does she?'

Mme Dupont shook her head, her smooth pink cheeks seeming to droop. Harriet was about to pursue the subject when Mme Dupont, at the bottom of the rucksack by now, pulled out the book of photographs of long-ago dancers and flopped herself down on to the bed with a thump, making Harriet bounce up and down.

'Regarde! Look at them! All danseurs de l'Opéra, n'est-ce pas? Qu'est-ce qu'ils sont moches! How ugly zey are!'

'Moche' seemed to cover a multitude of sins: disagreeable, ugly, anything unpleasant. Quite a useful word to remember, thought Harriet, especially for Jessica. She smiled to herself and craned over Mme Dupont's shoulder to look at the book lying on her ample lap. With little cries and giggles, and much jabbing of her finger, Mme Dupont dissected each dancer, each costume, each pose, till she flipped over a page to reveal Giuseppina Bozzacchi, kneeling in her tulle, the little foot peeping out, her long ringlets over her shoulder, her huge dark eyes looking down.

'Ooh, là. She is very beautiful, is she not?'

Suddenly a vivid memory struck Harriet of Marianne sitting, stiff and shaking, looking down at the photograph. Harriet paused and looked up. And then the crying . . . the sobs she had heard alone in the library. Had that simply been her imagination? She looked down again at the photograph, almost afraid of what she would see. Which way was Giuseppina facing? To the left. But which way should it have been? She shivered a little.

Mme Dupont looked up. ' 'Arriette? What is wrong?'

But, like her though she did, Harriet felt she did not know Mme Dupont well enough yet to tell her the story of Marianne dropping the book and running out of the library. She shook her head. 'Nothing. I think I'm just a bit tired, that's all and I – well, I just shivered for a minute. We call it a goose running over your grave . . .'

Mme Dupont asked no questions about the old saying but clapped a hand to her forehead and jumped up, letting out a stream of French. She took

Harriet by the hand and hauled her out of the room.

'You must eat, ma petite. What am I t'inking? A long journey. You are tired, 'ungry, n'est-ce pas? We must feed you and – and er . . . lie you in bed, non?'

'Well, something like that,' said Harriet with a grin and followed the old lady across the hall.

Mme Dupont pointed at a door next to Harriet's bedroom. 'Bat'room,' she said, 'you and me in zat one. Mlle Cantal, she is en suite. OK?'

Harriet nodded, relieved. For some reason she had worried about sharing a bathroom with Marianne's mother, but with Mme Dupont she couldn't imagine any embarrassment.

'Alors,' said Mme Dupont, throwing open the kitchen door. 'I will prepare for you une petite omelette and a salade de tomates. And frites? Cheeps?'

'Cheeps? Oh, chips – no. No, thank you. Not chips, but the rest would be brilliant. Thank you.'

Mme Dupont shrugged. 'Eh. No frites. Watching the figure, hein?' She sighed a deep sigh. 'Mlle Mireille. She don't never eat cheeps neither. Artistes. All zer same. Watch the figure. Watch the figure. I was like that once.' She patted her big round stomach and giggled. 'Too late now, hein?'

Harriet laughed. She sat at the big scrubbed kitchen table and put her chin in her hands while

Mme Dupont began to bustle about. She took eggs from a wooden stand and butter from a huge white fridge, unhooking pans and herbs from a beam overhead. Harriet could imagine such a kitchen in the country, but here in the city it seemed strange, especially since what she had seen of the rest of the apartment seemed so grand. Before she went to bed she would have a look round perhaps – unless Madame – no, Mademoiselle Cantal she must call her – came back.

'Where is Mlle Cantal?'

Mme Dupont threw her a disbelieving look. 'Where you t'ink? She at theatre.'

'She's a dancer too?'

'Non, non, non. Do you not know? You not 'eard of 'er? Mireille Cantal? She is great cabaret artiste. Very famous. Very beautiful. Very amusante. Very . . .' She shrugged, waving an egg whisk in her hand. Very everything it seemed. Harriet was even more nervous about meeting her now.

'When will she be home?' she said in a small voice.

'Ah. Later. After you in bed. She 'as television talk after zer show tonight.'

She made it sound as if a television interview after the show was an everyday thing. Perhaps it was. Harriet's head was in a whirl.

'You will not meet 'er till tomorrow,' said Mme Dupont. 'She will sleep in zer morning and I take you to l'Opéra so you not get lost, hein?'

Harriet nodded. Her eyes were beginning to feel heavy. Mme Dupont put a huge fluffy omelette and a delicious salad of tomatoes and herbs in front of her and stood over her while she ate it, every scrap. She cleaned her teeth in the shiny little bathroom, too tired to bother about yet more mirrors, and climbed into bed. What a day! Her first view of Paris, high kicks in the street, a proper French omelette, an apartment with a hall the size of a dance studio, and last, a fleeting thought of a young ballerina in white tulle kneeling modestly, her head bowed ... But almost before her head hit Marianne's lavender-smelling pillow, Harriet was fast asleep.

# *Chapter 7*

At the stage door of the Opéra, Mme Dupont handed Harriet over to the concierge like a precious parcel. With a hug, a smacking kiss on both Harriet's cheeks and a final admonitory wag of the finger to the concierge (who took no notice at all), she bustled away under a huge umbrella. The misty rain seemed to make the city softer and turned the sparkle into a gentle glow, so different from the damp, grey mist of London in the rain. Harriet leant out of the small door let into the giant dock doors and waved the old lady goodbye as she turned the corner and blew Harriet another kiss.

'À tout à l'heure,' she called. 'See you later.'

Harriet tried not to feel small again as she turned back and almost crept towards the cavernous hallway, past the concierge's room. Without Mme Dupont to bully him, the greasy-haired man in the green cardigan had lost interest in her completely and was leaning on a counter, watching a television high up in one corner, a mug of coffee in one hand.

She tried to remember how to get to the rehearsal studio, but between them, he and Mme Dupont had muddled her from the start. French words had batted back and forth between them at such a rate that she had felt like an onlooker at a ping-pong match, and now she stood in the hallway, stuck at the first hurdle. Corridors opened off the enormous dark space, stacks of scenery piled against one wall and smelling unpleasantly of dust and damp and old size, like rotten feet. She edged in a little further, her trainers shuffling over the uneven concrete floor. Which corridor had he said?

She had almost decided to swallow her pride and go back to ask him again, when there was a noise at the entrance behind her. She turned.

'Harry!'

Will! Thank goodness!

Ballet bag over his shoulder, he chaînéed towards her down the dark passage and dived into a high arabesque to pick up her hand and plant on it a noisy, wet kiss.

'À ma princesse, toi, alors!'

Harriet laughed, partly in relief, partly at sheer pleasure at seeing him. She gave him a shove.

'Will, shut up. Just because you're in Paris. I suppose you'll go on like this now for ever.'

He made a play of drying her hand with his sweatshirt.

'Moi? Don't think so, 'Arry dear. Don't know enough French.' He giggled. 'Now, tell. How was it chez Marianne? How was ze muzzaire?'

'I didn't see her. She was at some theatre somewhere. She's a big star, I was told.'

'Ah! A truly Big Fromage!'

'Hmm. I guess. Anyway, I get to meet her tonight. But the lady who looks after everything is great. Mme Dupont. She's really nice. Will, where's Marianne?'

Will's face clouded over.

'What's the matter? She's not ill? It's not Jessica?'

'No, no. Just – just a bit tired, I think. And she's not in the same room as Jessica so that's OK. Don't worry, Harry, I've kept my beadies on her. She's coming on later.'

'She'll miss class!'

Will shook his head. 'Miss McGregor's giving her a warm-up before we do the pas de deux. She'll be OK. She's not in any of the other pieces so . . .'

'Should I go and see her? See if she's all right?'

Will shook his head again. 'Stay cool, Harry. Leave her. She was asleep. She said the journey zonked her.

Come on. Come and watch class. The dressing-rooms are up here. We came over last night and had a quick peeky-boo.'

Harriet laughed and followed him as he burbled on, twirling his way along the narrow passageway. The other students crowded alongside, greeting her and babbling excitedly to each other. Halfway along, Will grabbed Harriet and hauled her to one side to a pair of double doors. For a moment she looked at him in amazement, but he hoiked her up on his chest to a small window set into the door and she peered through.

There in front of her was just one corner of the stage of the Opéra. Deserted and shadowy before the work of the day began, it seemed still but expectant, banks of lights hanging far overhead and ranged down metal poles on either side, glimpsed between towering ranks of curtains, blank and staring as if waiting to burst into life. Will gave Harriet another hoik and more of the stage came into view. So, so big! So amazing! Imagine dancing there!

'Put me down, Will,' she said in a small voice. The knowledge that she wouldn't be dancing there, not ever, washed over her.

'It's – it's not going to happen . . .' she said and couldn't manage any more. All those dreams she'd had – gone. Oh, she'd dance, she would dance somewhere, somehow, but never in a place like this the way she'd imagined it – and the dreams kept coming back and poking themselves into her mind, just when she thought she was coming to terms with reality.

'Oh, Harry,' said Will, suddenly understanding and hugging her to him for a moment. 'Harry, I'm so sorry. You're such a brilliant dancer. Why can't they see?'

'I'm a short, fat b-b-brilliant dancer, that's what,' said Harriet, sniffing and pushing him away. 'And I'll just have to get on with it. And – and I don't think I want to watch class.'

Will didn't say any of the usual things, but grabbed her hand and tugged her after him up the stairs. At the top he turned and said in a gritty voice, 'If you were that short and fat, Harriet *dear*, you wouldn't be here at all, would you? Would you?'

Harriet shrugged. No one kinder than Will at times, but no one like him to stop you feeling sorry for yourself. He rarely used that voice, but when he did . . .

He softened. 'It isn't fair, Harry, it really, really isn't fair, but . . .'

'I know,' she said, 'and this isn't exactly the

moment to get in a state about it either, but seeing all that . . .' She jerked her head down towards the pass-doors to the stage. Will gave a little 'Hmm'.

'Go and get changed, Will,' said Harriet. 'I'm OK. I will come and watch. Of course I will.' She sighed and rubbed her nose with the back of her hand. 'There's still stuff to learn, even watching. Where's the studio?'

'Two floors down. Wait in the girls' and I'll fetch you.'

'I'll wait down there,' she said, nodding towards the pass-doors again. She put her head on one side and pressed her lips together. 'Maybe I'll just have a little look inside.'

Will raised an eyebrow, pursed his own lips to hide a smile and nodded. He banged in through the dressing-room door and Harriet padded down the bare wooden stairs to the pass-doors. With a quick glance round, she opened them a crack and slid inside. There was no one about. She crossed the wide, dusty wings and crept between the heavy black velvet wing tabs, taking care not to knock against the pole with the lights. The full breathtaking size of the stage opened in front of her. It was gigantic. What you could do in a space like this!

Almost without thinking, she dumped her bag and

ran a few steps forward into a pirouette. She chasséed out of it, swung round, her arm curved over her head, and gasped. Her arm dropped to her side. The front of house curtain was raised and the red and gold of the vast auditorium glinted from the shadows, row upon row of empty seats, tier upon tier of empty boxes, balconies, to the very, very top where, in the centre, a huge crystal-dropped chandelier hung catching the light from the bare bulbs of the working rig. She stood transfixed.

The sudden sound of a door closing made her whirl round. Someone might be coming and she probably shouldn't be here. There might be trouble. She might even be sent home. What about Marianne then? In a panic, she ran to snatch up her bag, and as she stood up a flash of white caught her eye from the depths of the darkness in the wings opposite. She paused. One of the students already in costume? Bit early for that. A French dancer, maybe? One of the Petits Rats, the students at the Opéra school? Certainly not a techie; technicians wore black, not white.

A sudden cool draught seemed to come from across the stage and she took a step back. A door must have opened somewhere. The curtains on the far side swayed and beyond them a faint, pale light flickered.

She wanted to run, to get out of sight, but something made her wait a moment longer. As she watched, a small hand pulled back the curtain and the edge of a tulle skirt appeared, the frills transparent in the glimmer of light from behind them, a strand of skeleton leaves drifting down the front. Harriet held her breath.

'Who – who's . . .' Her voice was no more than a croak but whoever it was, was slowly starting to move towards her.

Somewhere a door banged. The hand was snatched away and the curtain fell back, swinging gently.

With a sudden chill, Harriet knew who it was over there in the shadows of the great theatre. She couldn't move, couldn't call out, but she knew . . . the girl in the photograph . . . Giuseppina Bozzacchi had been watching her.

But it was impossible. She pulled herself together. Enough of these mysteries – crying girls, moving photographs and now this . . . There must be some other explanation. But just as she made herself take a step forward towards the opposite wing to make sure, voices sounded behind her, catching her breath and making her jump. She scuttled into the wing nearest to the pass-doors and furthest from where the girl had been. She flattened herself against the curtain, clutching her rucksack to her chest, her eyes large, her breathing sounding loud. Two men sauntered on to the stage and more of the working lights flicked on.

She peered back across the expanse but the far wing was still in darkness with no sign that anyone had been there. Her head told her it couldn't have been and yet – only the hand and the edge of a skirt, but they had been enough to make her certain for a moment that it was her, Giuseppina, standing there.

The men's voices brought her to herself. They stood centre stage. Harriet recognized one as Mike Simms, Stage Director for the school production. He was looking round, craning his neck up at the web of gantries way above, then at the towers of lights in the wings. She edged away a little further before he should realize she was there, but her tiny movement drew his attention.

'Hey! What are you doing here?'

The man with him strode across to her, gabbling away in French.

'One of ours, I think,' said Mr Simms. 'Must've got lost, I daresay.' He moved towards her and she sidled out from the shelter of the curtain.

'Oh, you're the little extra one they told me about, aren't you?' he said. 'I saw you on the coach. I'm told you've got permission to watch the show from up here on stage but you shouldn't be here now – what's your name?'

'Harriet.'

'Shouldn't be here, Harriet, not without a member of the stage staff and not without permission, which I assume you – have – not – got. Not from me, anyway. Come on,' he said, firmly but not unkindly, 'off you go.' And he took her shoulder and propelled her gently towards the pass-doors, giving her a friendly wink as she went.

Outside, Will was frantically looking about.

'There you are. Harry, I'm going to be late. You shouldn't have gone in there, for goodness sake.' He paused for a moment. 'What were you up to? You look as if you've seen a— No don't tell me, I don't want to know if you're in trouble.'

Harriet followed him as he leapt down the stairs three at a time.

'I know, I know. I didn't mean . . .' but she ran out of breath chasing after him. She slipped into the studio to huddle behind the piano and Will hit the barre still running just as Miss McGregor started: 'À la seconde, demi plié – and . . .' She made a point of looking at her watch and then at Will as, round the edge of the studio, arms outstretched, the whole class sank down, rose and sank again into the first exercise.

The familiar sounds of the music, the swish and rhythmic pat of feet, the occasional flutter of sweat falling, should have been soothing. But behind the piano, Harriet couldn't concentrate. She remembered that she had brought the book of photographs with her in case there was time to do some research. Quietly, moving as little as possible so as not to draw attention to herself, she put her rucksack between her feet. By dint of looking up to watch and keeping absolutely still for long moments, by the time Miss McGregor was setting the second adage, Harriet finally managed to unzip the bag a bit at a time and slide the book out. She had put in a Post-it to keep the place, and the book opened at the picture of Giuseppina.

Giuseppina hadn't changed. She still knelt there, her eyes cast down, the bouquet at her foot, facing the way she had originally faced. Or so Harriet thought . . . The leaves were real leaves, not skeletons as they had seemed to be in the dim light of the stage, but they still drifted down the front of the tulle in exactly the same way. And those little hands clasped so demurely in front of her, so delicate, so soft, so white . . . Harriet gave herself a little shake. No ballerina's hands were big and red and clumsy, for heaven's sake. And this kind of costume was still worn in some of the great classics even now, *Coppélia* for instance, *La Fille Mal Gardée* . . .

But were those ballets on the programme for the Opéra company these days? And why was someone on stage at that hour of the morning in costume anyway? A wardrobe fitting perhaps? Someone just messing about? Very unlikely in a great company like this. But Giuseppina . . . ? Giuseppina was dead . . . And yet that little hand, those leaves . . . if only she had seen the face. If Mike Simms and the other guy hadn't come in just then, she was certain that whoever it was behind the curtain would have come towards her. Whoever it was had wanted to see *her*.

The class ended. Harriet closed the book and jumped up, putting thoughts of Giuseppina behind her. Rehearsals would begin after a short break, in the studio to start with, on the stage tomorrow. She crossed to Will to see what time he would be working with Marianne – but Jessica, towel round her shoulders, immaculate in her regulation lilac leotard, pushed in front of her. She dabbed affectedly at her forehead and fanned herself with the end of the towel. Harriet sighed loudly, rolling up her eyes.

Jessica's eyes flashed. 'What's happened to your

tubby friend, then – little miss Fatso? Too gross to dance, is she? That makes two of you.' She grimaced in a sickly-sweet smile of mock pity and swanned away with her cronies.

Harriet went white with rage and stamped through the studio doors, letting them bang behind her. Outside she kicked the wall, making her foot sting through the sole of her trainer. Miss McGregor followed her outside.

'Harriet, that will do. If you are going to cause trouble you will have to go home. Remember you're only here as a favour because Marianne's father has asked. Marianne will have enough to do without you stirring up trouble and distracting her.'

'But, Miss McGregor, I . . .'

'I mean it, Harriet. No trouble.' And Miss McGregor swept on down the passage to the stairs.

Harriet stood quite still and took a few deep breaths. Not fair. Just not *fair* – she clenched her fists and went to kick the wall again, but thought better of it. She hurtled down the stairs to the dark hallway at the entrance. At the end of the passage, one of the dock doors was open. Coming towards her she saw a figure silhouetted against the uncertain light. She stopped. The figure seemed to be almost transparent, a halo of light looking like tulle skirts swirling in the draught from the door, as it moved towards her raising a hand . . .

'Giusep—'

' 'Arry? Is that you?'

'Marianne!' Harriet let out a huge breath, flew over to her and threw her arms round her. Behind Marianne the dock door rattled shut.

'Marianne – are you OK? Will said—'

Marianne extracted herself, looking a little puzzled. 'Fine,' she said. 'I'm fine, 'Arry. Of course. What did you think?' She gave Harriet a weak smile. 'I'm – I'm just a bit tired, that's all.'

That's all? Harriet looked at her closely. Under the feeble, yellowish light bulb in the hallway, Marianne looked like death.

# Chapter 8

'Marianne!' Harriet blurted out. Why wasn't Marianne hurrying to get ready? It must be months since she'd seen her mother. 'Don't you want to see your mum?'

Rehearsal over, they stood outside the rehearsal studio in the passage. Away from the yellow light in the hallway below, Harriet had decided that Marianne looked a little better. Now, however, she just looked annoyed. 'Of course. Of course I want to see 'er, but I need a shower and I need to rest a little and—'

'But you could rest at home . . .'

' 'Arree,' said Will in a meaningfully cool voice. 'Don't be a nag now, duckie. She'll come when she's ready. Why don't *you* go out and have a look at Paris for an hour and then come back for Marianne?'

'On my own?'

'You're a big girl now, Harry.' His eyes suddenly

103

lit up. 'Why not Gucci down to the Grands Boulevards down the road there and indulge in a little wishful-thinking retail therapy? Hmm? Wish I could come too.'

Harriet glared at him. 'I don't do wish-therapy or whatever you call it,' she said. 'I'll just wait for Marianne till she's ready.'

Truth to tell, the idea of Paris on her own was a bit daunting and anyway, she wanted to be with Marianne to see all those exciting places out there for the first time. Even worse was the thought of going back to the apartment to meet Marianne's mother without her. She didn't quite understand why she had built up this feeling about Mlle Cantal, but even the thought of Mme Dupont didn't make it any easier to face Marianne's mother on her own.

Marianne wiped her neck and shoulders with her towel, hauled on her baggiest top and smiled at Will. 'That was not too bad, was it, Will?' she said.

'Non, non, chérie,' said Will adjusting his headband, not looking at her. 'It was fine.'

But Harriet knew that he was just being nice. The pas de deux had been rocky, one difficult passage in particular, and Alistair Mildmay had looked a bit worried at the end of the rehearsal. He had patted Marianne reassuringly on the arm as he left, saying not to worry, there were still a couple of days to go and everyone was bound to be a bit 'off' after the journey yesterday, but Harriet knew and she was sure Will knew too, that it was Marianne who was 'off', not Will. No one said so of course. Always the boy's fault. Harriet thought of Marianne's ashen face when she had come in earlier, and wished and wished Gareth was here with them.

Just then, Mike Simms stuck his head round the studio door.

'Hi,' he said, 'any of you guys want to come and take a look at the stage? Alistair and some of the others are there now and he says to come down if you like. You'll be on tomorrow afternoon for your first go, but you might as well see what you're in for.' He grinned. 'It's quite a sight. Makes the stage at home look like peanuts. Oh, hullo, Harriet.'

Harriet blushed a little but luckily he didn't say anything about her earlier visit to the stage in front of the few students still hanging about in the studio.

Will swept up his own bag and Marianne's. 'Try and stop me,' he said. 'Come on, La Marianna, let's go.'

They all trotted down the stairs to the pass-doors, where Harriet hung back, but Mike Simms gave her a little prod and a wink.

'Go on,' he said, 'my permission . . .' and he grinned some more.

On stage, Marianne was suddenly transformed. Her face took on a glow and a weight seemed to drop from her shoulders under their bulky sweatshirt. She looked round, turning slowly till she faced the huge empty auditorium, the red plush seats tipped up in their tiers, higher and higher, gazing down at her like rows of open eyes.

The people gathered on the stage went quiet, stepping back as she simply stood there, a little smile at the corner of her mouth. Quietly, Will put down the bags and stepped up behind her. He reached forward, gently took her hand and raised it over her head. Almost automatically, Marianne rose up on one pointe, extended the other leg high à la seconde and whipped into a double pirouette, landing securely in one of Alistair's strange, twisted positions. It was faultless: no hitches, no fumbles.

Will calmly lifted her and carried her across the wide space, tossed her up lightly and caught her by upper arm and thigh, spinning her low to the ground where she slid to earth, one leg stretched behind her, one arm reaching forward toward the empty auditorium. There was a little spatter of applause from the dancers watching and Alistair ran forward to take her hand and pull her to her feet.

'Perfect,' he said. 'You see? No worries. I knew you could do it.'

Marianne looked pleased and nodded. She reached up, pecked Will on the cheek and hurried over to Harriet. Harriet noticed Alistair give Will a pat on the back and a wide grin. So Alistair knew where the problem was. That was one of the lifts that had given such trouble in the studio and now Will had seized the moment, turned it to advantage and made it seem so easy. What a gem he was turning out to be.

Harriet turned to Marianne. 'OK now?' she said. 'See? Everyone knew it would be all right.'

Marianne nodded. 'I don't know why we couldn't get it when we were upstairs in the studio,' she said. 'But it is – like you say, it's OK now,' and she wrapped her towel round her shoulders.

'I'll take a quick shower and we will go to my mother's,' she said. 'You coming up or you want to wait 'ere?'

Harriet glanced round to see where Jessica might be. She saw her pirouetting like mad and, when she missed one, tossing her head with a loud, affected laugh and bending over, scuffing with her shoes as if they were to blame. She and her cronies looked as if they were going to be there for a while, flinging themselves about and generally showing off. Marianne would be all right in the dressing-room.

'Tell you what,' said Harriet. 'I think I'll wait outside. We've been cooped up here all day and someone said the rain had stopped.'

'OK,' said Marianne with a smile, 'see you,' and hurried through the doors. Harriet watched her go, wondering about her sudden change of mind, her sudden confidence about going home. Perhaps getting the lift right had made the difference. She stretched herself, holding her back, stiff from sitting all day. As she felt her spine crack with a satisfying pop, she pondered on Marianne's phrase 'go to my mother's'. She hadn't said 'home', had she? And yet her room was waiting, a bit bare and forsaken perhaps, but her bed and her books were still there. Harriet shook her head, perplexed, and turned to leave the stage.

Suddenly, she stood still, frowning. What – what was that? Surely someone was crying somewhere. She looked back at the dancers. They were quieter now. Jessica was sitting on the floor with Peter and one or two others. Some were marking steps, some looking out at the auditorium, shading their eyes against the working lights, brighter now than they had been this morning. No one was in distress that she could see. Mike Simms was chatting to the French Stage Director and Miss McGregor was beside them, joining in their discussion from time to time. They didn't seem concerned about anything.

But still she could hear the sound of weeping. Just like . . . just like it had been in the library. She bit her lip. After a moment, she moved quietly from the pass-doors along the darkened wing up to the back of the stage and peered round the long black velvet curtain that ran across the width of the space. A pale light at the far end in the opposite wing cast a shadow on the back wall. The shadow was still, just the outline of a girl in tulle skirts, her hair piled high and hanging in ringlets. Her head was bowed and she seemed to have her hands over her face. Harriet took a deep breath . . . Giuseppina. This time she was sure.

She started across the back of the stage in the dark, just seeing enough in the reflected light beyond to avoid pitfalls. She paused as the crying stopped. The girl lifted her head and whispered something in French. Harriet listened hard, but the voice was so faint and so loaded with tears she couldn't understand.

'Wait,' she whispered as she went, 'wait . . . I'm coming . . .'

But Mike Simms walked briskly into the far wing

from the stage and the light vanished. Harriet swore quietly under her breath. She was in pitch darkness now, shielded by towering black curtains. She stood still for a moment, then started to feel her way back the way she had come, her feet stumbling over cables anchored to the floor with gaffer tape, stubbing her toe on a stage weight. She stood still again, letting her eyes get used to the gloom.

After a moment, more working lights flooded on round her and she fled round the curtain into the wings and burst through the double doors. She stopped herself at the top of the stairs, grabbing the metal rail. Holding on, she rocked backwards and forwards on the lip of the step, feeling the wood hard against the arch of her instep through her trainers, strangely comforting in the midst of all the muddle she felt.

What had that sad, sad voice been trying to say? It had sounded so urgent, words tumbling out through sobs. It was Giuseppina. But how could it be? If anyone had asked her, Harriet would have said she didn't believe in ghosts. But then, if anyone had asked her, she would have said it was impossible for anything to come between her and Marianne – that she could have talked to her about anything.

Suddenly, the mystery of Giuseppina and the

problem of Marianne seemed intertwined.

Harriet slid on to the next step, gripping the rail and landing with a flop, and went on down the stairs. At the bottom, she walked out through the shadowy hallway, past the concierge's room, and out into the sunshine. She stood in the street outside. Anxiety about Marianne, anxiety about Giuseppina, all went churning through her mind.

She paced up and down, hardly noticing the open slatted window-shutters where women leant through and chatted to others on the pavement, the baskets of long baguettes and gorgeous pastries in the yeasty-smelling boulangerie close by, the old man walking a little dog from lamppost to lamppost.

At last Marianne came out through the doors, her hair still damp from the shower.

'I know,' she said with a smile, 'let's go to my mother's through the Galeries. 'You can't go 'ome without seeing Les Galeries, il le faut – you must.'

'Galeries? What's that?' said Harriet, thinking of their visits to art galleries with the school at home.

'Department store. Enormous. Magnifique. You can't imagine. Come.' Marianne seemed animated and alive now, not like the little dead thing that had arrived this morning. Harriet seized the idea eagerly. Anything to take her mind off ghosts and starving dancers – and anyway her first French department store would be something to tell her mum about.

'Brilliant!' she said. 'Chouette *alors*, in fact.' Marianne laughed at her terrible accent, but Harriet grabbed her arm. 'Best I can do,' she said. 'Let's go.'

They set off down the street and out into the busy boulevard, leaving the regal steps and columns and statues of the Opéra façade behind them. A little further on there was a stall selling pancakes. Harriet stopped and held Marianne's sleeve as she watched the woman pouring the thick, sticky mixture on to the sizzling plate, where it spread and bubbled. She squeezed a lemon over it and sprinkled it with something heady from a bottle. It smelt delicious.

'Oh, Marianne,' said Harriet, sniffing luxuriously. 'Let's have one. Go on, one won't hurt us.'

Marianne looked almost panic-stricken.

'Go on,' said Harriet. 'I bet you didn't get breakfast, getting up late like that at the hostel.'

'Non, non,' said Marianne, angrily, 'of course I get – got breakfast. I had chocolat and a croissant on the way at a café. I did, 'Arry, I did.'

Now Harriet knew she was lying. She was protesting too much. And she might have had coffee, but chocolate, never. She bit her lip and then said as sternly as she could manage, 'Marianne, don't tell me porkies. I know you and there's no way you had chocolate. I know you didn't.'

Marianne went red and pulled away roughly. 'I am not liar,' she said, her voice tight with fury. 'And *don't* say that I am. Go away, 'Arriet. You are not my friend if you say I lie.'

Harriet followed her and took her arm, but she wrenched it away and stalked off. Harriet hurried after her, took her arm again and turned the angry girl towards her. She took both her shoulders and looked into her eyes, but Marianne dropped her gaze.

'Marianne, listen to me. Of course I'm not calling you a liar. Don't be daft. Please. Calm down, will you – just listen.' She put an arm round her shoulders, feeling them thin and bony even through the big sweater. 'Listen. You're in a state with all this going on,' she jerked her head back towards the great façade of the Opéra behind them. 'I do understand, I do. And don't say I'm not your friend, because I am. But, Marianne, you must eat or—'

'I did eat, I did – not . . . not chocolat but I did eat . . .' Marianne was almost in tears now.

'OK, I believe you. I do, honestly,' said Harriet. There mustn't be a row, and anyway, it was useless to argue, better just to try to get Marianne to swallow something, anything, right now. Marianne seemed to cool down a little.

'But, please,' Harriet went on, 'it's my first time in Paris. And I want to do everything, see everything.' She gave a little laugh she didn't feel like. 'Even eat everything. And I want to do it with you. Come on, Marianne. Just for me. Couldn't you manage a pancake so I don't feel lonely?' She smiled again, knowing it must look forced, but Marianne softened and gave her a hug.

'All right,' she said, 'just for you, 'Arry. We will have crêpes going along the street comme les gamines, and we will go to the Galeries before we go . . .' and her face darkened for a moment '. . . before we go . . .'

'Home?' said Harriet.

'Oui,' said Marianne, 'chez ma mère.'

They munched their pancakes, hot and oozing syrup in little paper packets, licking their lips and giggling as they went, Harriet relieved that their quarrel was over and that Marianne was eating. They sucked their fingers, put the papers in a bin outside the big glass doors of the Galeries and went inside.

Harriet laughed with delight at the Aladdin's cave in front of them. She wanted to stop and look at everything – perfumery, hand bags, jewellery, scarves

– but Marianne threaded her way quickly to the foot of the giant escalator that ran up through the building. She looked at the store guide.

'Ugh,' she said, giving her fingers another lick, 'I am still sticky. I need to wash my hands.' She put her foot on the escalator and began to soar upwards. With a sigh, Harriet followed, her heart sinking. Wash her hands? Was that all? Would Marianne really go as far as to throw up in such a public place? Harriet looked up at the set of the shoulders under their thick sweater, gliding up the escalator ahead of her, and shook her head. Of course she would. Marianne would do just what she wanted and nothing Harriet could say would stop her.

# Chapter 9

Harriet lay under Marianne's quilt unable to sleep, her conscience troubling her. Why had she decided not to follow Marianne into the Ladies in the Galeries? She had told herself it was so as not to spy, to prove to herself she trusted Marianne. But was it really just because everything was getting on top of her? She truly hoped it wasn't that.

But lying there in the dark, she knew there had been a bit of that about it. As she tossed and turned, she told herself the Ladies in a big department store would have been noisy with running water, toilets flushing, chat and the rattle of plastic bags, so she probably would have been none the wiser anyway. But the joy of the outing was gone for her – both in the reality then, and in the memory of it now. When Marianne had returned, they had gone on round the huge store, but try though she did, Harriet had no heart for it. After a while, Marianne had looked at her and said, 'Let's go, 'Arry. You 'ad enough, hm? Let's go to my mother's then.'

Harriet closed her eyes to blot out the memory with sleep, but sleep wouldn't come. She lay thinking about the evening that had followed. Mme Dupont had been overjoyed to see them, and Harriet had felt really included, especially as Mme Dupont made the effort to speak English all the time she was there. She had hugged Marianne tight and then patted her cheeks, her shoulders and arms before enfolding her in another hug and fussing her to the table.

'Maman is resting,' she said to Marianne. 'We will not wake 'er yet, hein?' and Marianne had shaken her head. She nibbled at the salad Mme Dupont made and wrinkled her nose when she was scolded for her lack of appetite.

'Like when I was little,' she said to Harriet with a chuckle. 'She always bullied me like that, 'Arry. You see, it 'as not changed. To 'er I'm still a baby.' And Mme Dupont clucked, her pink cheeks wobbling into a fond smile.

They talked of the performance, of Gareth nursing his sore shoulder in London and of Will-the-hero. There was a short demonstration of a step or two from the pas de deux with Harriet and Marianne giggling as they got it all wrong, and Mme Dupont insisting on trying a pirouette or two on uncertain, chubby legs, making them giggle even more. Then, suddenly serious again, they told Mme Dupont a bit about Jessica and her nasty ways, leading to more clucking of an indignant kind.

'Qu'est-ce qu'elle est moche alors,' she said.

'Yes,' said Harriet, 'absolutely moche, moche, moche,' and nodded energetically. Beside her, Marianne smiled, sitting at the big scrubbed table, twiddling with a basil leaf and sniffing her fingers, half-closing her eyes with pleasure. She drank a large cup of black coffee and, to Harriet's surprise, took a thin galette biscuit to go with it. But soon after, she went to the bathroom and Harriet swung round, following her with her eyes, a worried frown on her face.

Mme Dupont looked at her. ' 'Arriette?'

Harriet swivelled back and leant her elbows on the table. She shook her head and shrugged her shoulders. 'I don't know what to do.'

'She does not eat, non?'

'She – does – not – eat – non,' she said, shaking her head hard in time with the words. 'I can't prove it. She *says* she does. But it's always somewhere else, some other time, never with me. She hates the canteen food, she says. But – but . . .'

Mme Dupont began to clear the table. 'She is too much thin, chérie. I know a dancer must be slim – I know 'er mother could not be . . .' She heaved a great sigh.

Harriet looked up. 'Will she listen to you? Marianne, I mean.'

Mme Dupont shrugged a 'no'.

'Could we talk to her mother? To Mlle Cantal?'

'Hm. Not you, 'Arriette, but I could try per'aps. It is more – well – 'er mother used to be – I t'ink she will not—' She cut herself off quickly and sighed again, went to the door and listened. There were sounds of movement across the hall.

'Écoute . . . I think Mademoiselle is awake now. She will come in. Say nothing, hein? I will – I will try later, maybe. But not now, not with Marianne 'ere. They are—' She shook her head hastily as Marianne left the bathroom and other footsteps sounded faintly across the hall. Harriet heard Marianne say in a small voice: 'Maman,' and another, deeper, velvety voice respond: 'Ah! C'est toi, Marianne.' But the voice was cool, nor was there the sound of hugging or kissing nor any other noises that said 'pleased to see you' in the way her own mother would.

The tall, elegant figure of Mlle Cantal entered the room, wrapped in satin and lace, her hand in the small of Marianne's back, ushering her before her almost like a herald. She held herself very upright, her large blue eyes looking down at both Marianne and Harriet, blinking a little, the eyelashes heavy with mascara. Her immaculate blonde hair was swept over to one side and she smelt of expensive scent. She held out a languorous hand to Harriet, but when she shook it, the grip was surprisingly firm, leaving the imprint of her rings on Harriet's fingers.

'You are Marianne's friend.' It was a statement, not a question. At least Mlle Cantal spoke perfect English, with hardly a trace of an accent.

Harriet looked at Marianne and smiled. 'Yes,' she said, 'I'm Marianne's friend.'

'Good. Well, Mme Dupont will look after you. Just ask for anything you need.'

'Thank you.' Was that all that was to be said about her visit? Like being in a hotel?

'Marianne, you are staying at this *hostel* place?' The beautifully made-up forehead creased into the vestige of a frown.

'Yes, Maman. The school say I must.'

A slight shrug of the shoulders under the silk dressing-gown.

'I see. You are doing a new pas de deux, yes?'

'Yes.'

They were talking as if they were strangers, thought Harriet. 'She's brilliant in it,' she said quickly to fill the gap. 'Are you coming to see it?'

Mlle Cantal ran the tip of her tongue over glossy lips. Harriet had a nasty feeling she had said the wrong thing, but the woman simply said, 'When is it, Marianne? What day did you say?'

'Saturday afternoon,' she said, with a sigh. 'Don't you remember?'

'Of course,' said her mother irritably. 'But you know how busy I am, chérie. One forgets these things. Well, I will see, but I have an interview with a journalist in the morning and it may run on, you know how it does.'

'Yes,' said Marianne, dropping her head, 'I know how it does.'

Mlle Cantal pursed her lips and gave a little shrug. 'Don't sulk now, Marianne. I will come if I can. Of course.' She turned, tapped to the door in her high-heeled silver mules, and turned back.

'Sylvie,' she said to Mme Dupont. 'I have no show tonight but I have to go out. I will have just a plain biscotte and a café noir. I will take it in my room.' She swept out, but not before Harriet had noticed that from behind Mlle Cantal did not look as svelte as she did from the front. The back of the dressing-gown clung a little, showing faint lines of underwear on quite a broad bottom. A tie-belt was pulled so tightly that the soft fabric bulged out above the waist. It was with relief that Harriet heard Mlle Cantal's door shut firmly across the hall. She looked at Marianne.

Mme Dupont stood by the table with her hand round Marianne's shoulders. She pressed her gently down on to a chair, muttering something soothing in French. Marianne's jaw clenched and her nostrils flickered. She clasped her hands in front of her on the table, the fingers in tight knots. Mme Dupont bent down and pressed her cheek to Marianne's and then rubbed the sharp white line of her cheekbone with one finger, still crooning quietly in French.

*Imagine having her as a mother*, thought Harriet. *Qu'est-ce qu'elle est more than moche. She's – she's, well . . . not – very – nice.* She thought with a sudden longing of her own mother in Sheffield, glad that she wasn't rushing off to cabarets every night. If Harriet had been dancing at the Opéra, even if only in the corps de ballet, she knew her mother would have dropped everything to see her. She'd have gone without things for herself to get there, too. She sat beside Marianne and drew a deep breath, wondering what to say.

Marianne seemed to sense her unease. She gave a harsh little laugh. 'Don't worry, 'Arry. She is always like that. We are used to it, aren't we, Sylvie?'

Mme Dupont straightened up and started foraging in a packet for French toasts. She banged around a bit with a tray, laying it with little pots of butter and jam. As well as a cafetière of black coffee, Harriet noticed a tiny jug of cream and some brown sugar. She caught Mme Dupont's eye and the old lady shrugged, turning up one corner of her mouth in a wry smile. Harriet bit her lips to stop a giggle. So Mlle Cantal told herself she was on a diet, with her 'just a black coffee and a biscotte', but Mme Dupont knew better and found it 'amusant' too.

Beside her, Marianne was calmer. 'It is true, 'Arry, Maman is always busy. She is a great artiste, you know. She sing – sings in theatre, in cabaret, film sometimes. I am – I am very proud of 'er.' Marianne's eyes sought Harriet's and Harriet gave a little nod.

'Of course you are,' she said, wondering why Marianne had never mentioned it before.

Mme Dupont took the tray along the passage and was gone for several minutes. Harriet heard the far door positively bang and her feet slap angrily on the parquet floor as she returned. She put an arm round Marianne and pulled her up from the table.

'If Maman cannot come on Saturday, I will come,' she said. 'Can I get a ticket?'

'Bien sûr, Sylvie – of course you will come anyway. I already 'ave – have two seats for family.' Mme Dupont looked pleased at that 'family'.

'Chouette! 'Ooray!' she said. 'I look forward. Will I sit wit' 'Arriette?'

Harriet shook her head. 'I'm allowed to watch from the wings,' she said.

'Excellent! We will meet after to – 'ow you say, chin waggle about it, hein?' She glanced at the kitchen clock. Ten past nine. 'Oh là! Regardez l'heure! Marianne, you must get back to your 'ostel? Oui. I call taxi.'

'Non, non, it isn't far. I can walk.'

'Pas à cette heure, Marianne – not so late.'

'It's not late, Sylvie. I will be fine.'

'Non. Taxi or you stay 'ere. You should be in bed early and I would not rest with you out there toute seule, all alone.'

'I'll walk with her if you like,' said Harriet.

'And then you walk back on *your* own and I worry about *you*. Très, *très* bien.' Mme Dupont gave her a mock-exasperated look, wagging her head, then turned to Marianne. 'If you promise to go at once in bed when we get there, 'Arriette and I will go wit'

124

you and come back together. 'Ow would that be, hein?'

Marianne smiled and Harriet jumped up, delighted. Paris at night. They would pass the Opéra all floodlit. She had seen postcards. Marianne picked up her bag and went into the hall. Mme Dupont nodded towards the closed door of Mlle Cantal's room.

'Tu vas – you will say au revoir to Maman?'

Marianne nodded and knocked gently at the door. 'Oui?'

'I am leaving, Maman.'

'Au 'voir, chérie. Come by tomorrow. I will be in, I think.'

Mme Dupont sniffed, her eyebrows raised. Marianne took her hand from the door handle and called 'Au 'voir' in a small voice. Her head dipped, she opened the door of the apartment and they went out, down the staircase out through the courtyard, and set off in the deepening twilight towards the Grand Boulevard.

There was the Opéra flooded in golden light, the great statues on the skyline greeting the stars with their upraised wings, the huge columns at the top of the steps giving glimpses of glittering chandeliers inside, more columns, more stairs with crimson carpets and heavy, round, pink polished stone banisters that curved away out of sight upwards to more splendours. Marianne and Harriet ran up the steps and peered in through the heavy glass of the doors, their noses pressed flat, nudging each other with excitement at the riches within.

As they ran down again, Harriet noticed a billboard advertising the school performance. There was a large coloured photograph of a class with Marianne at the front of the barre, her leg in a high seconde, her arm curved over her head, looking wonderful. Harriet slung her arm round Marianne's shoulders and gave her a hug.

'See?' she said. 'That's where you'll always be. In front, looking great, on posters everywhere.'

Marianne just shook her head, but Mme Dupont 'ooh là'd' with great pride, clapping her hands and looking round to see who was looking. Since nobody was, she bustled them off towards the darker streets that led away from the great building.

They delivered Marianne to the hostel and hurried home, with just a passing glance at the billboard on the way. Once in the apartment, Harriet was sent off to bed as Mme Dupont had 'things to do' and Harriet must be off early to watch class next day.

As she lay under the quilt unable to sleep, thinking

about all that had happened since she had arrived: the poster, the pas de deux, Marianne, what to do about her, she heard voices in the hall. Raised voices. She lay trying not to listen even though it was all in French. But then she heard Mme Dupont say 'Marianne'. Harriet sat up. Mlle Cantal was shouting, almost screaming, and something banged down hard on the hall table, making it rattle. Mme Dupont's voice came back, calmer, trying to stay controlled but interrupted by the anger bubbling out of Mlle Cantal. Harriet slipped to the door and opened it a crack, hoping it wouldn't make any sound.

The row went on but all she managed to pick up were the words 'Marianne' and, she thought, 'maigre', 'maigrir', thin, getting thinner, but the rest she couldn't understand. Mme Dupont was trying her best, she was certain, but Mlle Cantal wasn't listening, too angry to hear.

Suddenly the voices stopped and the front door slammed hard, even making the cupboard doors in her little room shake. Harriet slipped back into bed and put her head under the quilt. She was trembling a little, and pulled herself into a tight little ball, knees almost to her chin, hugging her stomach, feeling horrible, sad and guilty that she felt so helpless.

For a moment she wished she was at home in her

own safe little bed in Sheffield, far away from all these strange people and their strange voices, but gradually her eyes went heavy. Her last thought was a sudden faint image of a white hand on a towering black velvet curtain, gone before she could reach it. Someone was trying to tell her something … someone was trying … but the someone was carried away by the sleep that drifted over her, and she never got to hear.

# *Chapter 10*

The black cloud still sat on Harriet's shoulder in the morning. She felt heavy and her legs felt weak, as if she'd never dance again. She nibbled at a croissant, hot and crispy and delicious, but pushed it away.

'Oh là,' said Mme Dupont, ' 'Arriette. This will not do. You must not catch the disease of Marianne.'

Harriet gave a wan little smile. 'I don't think it's catching,' she said. 'Don't worry.'

'What is wrong?'

'I – oh, I don't know.'

Mme Dupont sat beside her and took her hand. 'You are worried about Marianne?'

Harriet nodded.

'But it is not just that, I t'ink, non? Come. Tell me.'

'Well, it's just that – I feel – I feel a bit out of place, somehow. You know. Just watching class and rehearsals and then, you know, watching the show from the wings. I mean, that's great but still sort of, something and nothing . . '

'You want to be part of it.' Mme Dupont patted her hand. 'It is 'ard, chérie. I understand. Truly, I do. I was very ill once, when I was young, and I could not dance for a long time. It was – eh . . . I still remember the pain of it. But now you 'ave the feeling it is for ever, hein?' She looked up at the kitchen clock. 'What time is the class?'

'Ten thirty. I said I'd see Marianne before.'

'Hmm. Attends.' She heaved herself up from the table, went to a pile of newspapers and magazines stacked on a dresser in the corner and rummaged among them. 'Voilà!' she said triumphantly, and made a brave attempt at a little couru back to the table, holding up a small booklet in front of her between dainty fingers. Harriet smiled.

'That's better, ma petite. Let us see if we can keep that smile, oui?' She put the booklet on the table.

'Studio Goncourt. Cours de danse,' read Harriet. 'That means dance classes, doesn't it?' she said, looking up at Mme Dupont.

'These classes are ouvertes au public . . .'

'Open to the public. To everyone. We've got places like that in London. I go sometimes on a Saturday if there's nothing happening at school.' She looked up eagerly. Mme Dupont took the booklet and flicked through it.

'I am a little – 'ow do you say – beyond the times now, but I know somet'ing about who is a good teacher and who is not. I 'ear such things, you know from old friends who 'ave granddaughters. Let me see . . . Ah oui!' She jabbed a finger at a photograph in the booklet. 'That one. 'E is good – Monsieur Bernard. 'E teached – er, taught – at the Opéra. 'E has a class at eleven hours. What do you t'ink, hein?'

'Oh, yes, yes please!' Harriet pushed back her chair and sprang up eagerly, but then her face fell. 'Is it very expensive – I mean, how much does it cost? I haven't got very much money with me and—'

'Tah-t-t-t-t! Sssh.' Mme Dupont held up an imperious finger. 'This will be my treat to the little friend of Marianne,' she said. 'Now. I will 'ear no argy-bargy. We will go together, to make sure you get there safe and to pay le Maître. Now, do you 'ave clothes – shoes – all that is nécessaire?'

Harriet blinked away sudden unbidden tears and nodded. 'Oh, thank you, Mme Dupont, thank you. Yes. Yes, I did bring my dance stuff,' she said with a little grin and hugging up her shoulders, 'just in case – just in case *they* changed their minds.'

Mme Dupont clapped her hands. 'Excellent,' she cried. 'It is a long, long time since I went to do class. It will bring back old days just to go inside and 'ear the piano, smell the smells – you know?'

Harriet did know. She knew exactly. She ran to the bedroom, shoved her ballet things into her bag and hurried back into the kitchen, her face suddenly anxious.

'Now what, ma petite?'

'Umm. I must tell Marianne where I am. And afterwards, er – how will I get to the Opéra – is it far? Will I have to go on the Undergr— I mean, the Métro – or what?'

'I will wait for you. There is always a café in these places, is there not? Then I will bring you à l'Opéra in time for re'earsal in the afternoon. It is not far. And we will go past the stage door on the way, so Marianne she know where you are.'

Harriet nodded, feeling a bit guilty that this hadn't been her first thought. Will had said he would make sure Marianne got to the Opéra without any Jessica trouble. But would Marianne mind her not being there for class? She thought not. Rehearsal was different, but she would be back in plenty of time for that. She scribbled a note to leave at the stage door for Marianne, while Mme Dupont scribbled another, slapped it down on the kitchen table and weighted it down with a sugar-sifter.

'Mademoiselle will not be awake for many hours yet. She sleep late, hein? But better I leave this – what you say? – in the case? Oui, in the case she wake up.'

Just to make sure Mademoiselle didn't waken, they crossed the hall on tiptoe and gently clicked the apartment door shut behind them.

The Studio Goncourt was bright, cheerful and full of bustle, the kind of people going and coming that Harriet was used to: young, slender and fit, straight-backed, smooth-haired, feet turned out as they rushed about late for class, or stood idly and elegantly waiting for friends, taking glances at themselves in the mirrors that lined the reception area. And the boys: some, like Gareth, tall and lithe; others like Will, flamboyant and dizzy. Although a bit shy because she knew no one, Harriet still had a feeling of 'coming home' as soon as they stepped inside the door. Mme Dupont went up to the reception desk.

After a few moments, she turned to Harriet, her face clouded.

'Monsieur Bernard is ill and his deputy cannot give the class today. Oh, 'Arriette, I am sorry, ma petite.

There is only one other class at this time and it is not classique – not what you are used to, I t'ink. It is more contemporain – you understand? Jazz contemporain.'

'It's Lee Washington,' said a voice behind them in English. 'He's brilliant. He's worked with Harlem and Joffrey and he's choreographing and giving class over here for a while. Go on, give it a go. Pity to miss it.'

Harriet looked round, looked up and up again. A young woman looked down at her, smiling, hair like a lively yellow bush, face as lean as a whippet. Harriet thought for a moment.

'I've done a little bit of contemporary but . . .'

'I know, a swan, a swan, and only a swan,' said the girl, her dark eyes laughing. 'I was too, till I hit six feet. Come on, you'll love it. Lee's really great.'

Mme Dupont looked doubtful but then nodded. 'Why not?' she said. 'Better than nothing, hein?'

Harriet gave her a quick kiss on the cheek. 'You sure you don't mind waiting? I mean, I think I can remember the way back . . .'

'Non, non. I will be 'appy to wait 'ere. Like old times. I don't want for you to get lost, 'Arriet.'

'Oh, thank you, Mme Dupont, you're really, really kind. I—'

'Off wit' you, or you will be late.'

The old lady gave Harriet a gentle shove, and she followed the tall girl into the changing room. Other people were wearing baggy track-suit bottoms and ragged tops, much more relaxed than her uniform leotard, and she didn't even have any footless tights. She did her hair in a ponytail and bundled on a sweatshirt top, ankle warmers and some soft shoes. She gave a quick look in the mirror. She still looked 'classy-ahsical' but not too out of place, she hoped.

The tall girl grinned down at her. 'You from London?'

Harriet nodded. 'Just here for a couple of days,' she said.

'I thought I recognized the leotard,' said the girl. 'I was at the Brit till I outgrew them.' The British Academy was a rival school, always known as 'the Brit', attached to another company in London. The girl grinned again. 'I guess you're at the other end of the scale,' she said, looking down at Harriet. Harriet nodded grimly.

'Not the end of the world,' said the girl. 'There's life after swans. I'm in cabaret here, but I do lots of different classes and there are small companies around that I work with. Cabaret keeps me going, while we do the proper stuff when we can. Really interesting work, experimental, you know? It's great.'

Harriet said nothing but nodded as if she did know.

'My name's Rosalie,' said the girl.

'Harriet,' said Harriet. She followed Rosalie into a big studio lined with mirrors over black walls, where a musician was putting out a set of percussion instruments in one corner.

'That's Jaimé,' said Rosalie. 'He's brilliant too.'

She turned away and greeted one or two other dancers sprawled on the floor, all of them in messy tops and holey tights, their hair gelled and spiky or caught back in a scrunchy with loose tendrils; all of them, Harriet noticed with interest, different sizes and shapes. Casually, they stretched different bits of themselves, holding their feet or knees, reaching behind them with their hands clasped, regarding themselves critically in the mirror, groaning and moaning all the time about how stiff they were as they sat in the splits or lifted a leg way above their head and gave it an extra pull. It was clear that, 'wrong' shapes or not, novices had no place in this class, as they sometimes did in the free classes she had been to in London. She dropped to the floor and joined in the grunt and heave, happier than she'd felt for days.

Rosalie turned back to her. 'So what are you doing here?' she said. 'Are you anything to do with that performance at the Opéra your lot are doing?'

Harriet's head ducked. 'Mmyes,' she said, 'sort of . . .'

Rosalie smiled a question.

'I'm just over for the ride,' said Harriet with a self-deprecating shrug. 'My friend's dancing a lead and she wanted me around, so . . .' She looked up at Rosalie squarely. 'I'm too short for the company, so I'm too short for this performance,' she said, in as matter-of-fact a way as she could manage.

Rosalie nodded. 'Been there, done that,' she said. 'Oh well. Best come and join us then. You're too short for cabaret too, but there's lots of other things going on. Small companies, solo work, all sorts. More than in London, I think, these days. Worth a try, huh?'

Somewhere inside, it felt as if a door had opened just a crack. Maybe, maybe . . .

Jaimé brushed a cymbal and struck it softly. Harriet looked up as a tall black man, all sinew and muscle, his head shaved and an earring in one ear, walked in and dumped his bag on a chair by the mirrored wall.

'Hi, guys. The day is ours. Let's move those beautiful bodies the way the good Lord intended.'

Lee Washington turned and the whole class sat up

137

and seemed to lift in expectation. He eased off his shoes, unfolded himself down on to the floor in one long, easy movement.

'OK, cool, let's go . . .'

Jaimé struck a single note on a high drum, picked up a rhythm on another, and without a word, the class began. Harriet struggled to keep up with the exercises that everyone seemed to know, but the atmosphere of utter concentration and the coming together of the rhythms crept into her, sweeping her along. Once they were on their feet and the exercises were set and not memorized, she relaxed, and when the jumps began and the rhythm slowed for the boys, without thinking, she worked with them. Even with an unfamiliar style, the familiar feeling of taking flight took over. Sweat pouring down her face and back, she kept with them, forgetting everything as the only reality became the quiet intensity of the room, the strange rhythms and the steps that let her soar. She was unaware of Lee's eyes watching her closely as her set swept across the floor.

After the class he beckoned her over as she wiped herself down with her towel. She glanced round to be sure he meant her, surprised to be singled out. But perhaps he greeted any new student this way.

'See you tomorrow?' he said in an American-drawled French accent.

Harriet shook her head sadly. 'I'm only here till Saturday and I haven't got any more money.'

'No sweat. Have one on me,' he said. She looked up at him. Did he really mean that? She could come for nothing? He smiled. 'Sure,' he said. 'You're good. Kinda little, but good. See you tomorrow.'

He picked up his bag and left, raising a hand towards Jaimé in salute. Harriet watched him go, open-mouthed. 'Kinda little, but good.' Good enough to come to his brilliant class for nothing? Really? As good as that?

'Thank you,' she whispered finally to the closing door, 'I – er, thank you . . .'

In the changing room, Rosalie seemed to look at her with new respect and a couple of the French dancers spoke to her but gave up when she didn't understand them, just grinning, nodding and holding up a thumb. She ran out to Mme Dupont, sitting patiently in the little café, surrounded by pot plants, a line of coffee cups in front of her.

'So?'

'It was – it was wonderful,' said Harriet. 'And I can come back tomorrow for nothing. Can you imagine?'

'Oui, chérie,' she said, beaming, 'I can imagine.

Très très bien. You see? Not the end of the world, l'Opéra.'

'No, not the end of the world. "Life after swans",' said Harriet, with a grin at Rosalie who was just leaving. Rosalie gave her a wave, but Mme Dupont just looked puzzled. Harriet gave up trying to explain just what 'life after swans' meant. She'd tell Marianne and Will later.

Marianne! They'd be late. They'd left the note, but she didn't want Marianne to feel abandoned. 'We must go,' she said, with a tug at Mme Dupont's sleeve. Mme Dupont nodded and picked up her bag, hastily stuffing into it the magazine she had been reading.

They hurried through the streets to the Grand Boulevard and round the corner of the Opéra building to the stage door, where the concierge was still watching the television. Harriet hugged Mme Dupont good-bye and ran inside and up the stairs. In her head she was still flying through the air to Jaimé's drums and bells and cymbals at the Studio Goncourt, and couldn't wait to tell Marianne and Will about it.

But as she passed the pass-doors to the stage, she heard other music. She hesitated. Were they rehearsing already? Marianne wasn't due on stage till two, and it was only half past one. Perhaps they were doing something else? But with a full orchestra? She pushed open the door and a blast of sound set her back on her heels.

*Coppélia!* The orchestra was playing the music for the grand pas de deux from Act III of *Coppélia*. She knew it well. They'd learnt parts of it in class and then she'd listened to it over and over as part of the research on the making of the ballet, when she'd first come across Giuseppina Bozzacchi. It wasn't part of the matinée programme, so why were they playing it now? Perhaps an Opéra ballet rehearsal was going on. If one of the French ballerinas was working, it would be really interesting to see her just for a minute. With a quick look round to see if Mike Simms was about, she slipped inside. She crept forward into the wings and peered towards the stage.

There was no one. The stage and the orchestra pit were in darkness. Just one small light crept around the stage, following the pattern of a dance, following a dancer who wasn't there . . .

Harriet drew a quick breath, then steadied herself. Perhaps it was a lighting rehearsal with a recording played over the tannoy. She made herself stand still. No, the music was here, all around her, resounding through the vast empty space as only a full orchestra can. No longer the familiar piece she knew, but somehow off-key, sinister now, it went on and on, swirling round her head, making her shiver. *Stop! Please stop!* She covered her ears, unable to move. The single light on the stage grew brighter, swinging across, up, down, faster and faster till suddenly it died and, in a discordant jangle, the music faded away.

Harriet looked across at the far wing. In a dim glow from somewhere behind it, she saw the black curtain move a little, there was a flash of white and all was still. She backed away, pushed through the pass-doors and, still shaking, bolted up the stairs.

# Chapter 11

Outside the studio, Harriet stopped and pulled herself together. What she had heard must have been a techie trying out the tannoy system with a CD that anyone in this place might have had hanging about. The curtain swinging and the flash of white? In the dark, she must have been mistaken. There had been no figure there, no hand on the curtain, and the faint glow would have come from the exit light beyond. She'd had too much excitement for one day, that was what it was. She needed to concentrate on Marianne now. Anything else could wait till later.

There were voices in the studio already and when she peeped through the circular glass at the top of the door, Marianne was there with Alistair, talking earnestly. Harriet took off her trainers, slipped through the door and, keeping to the side of the room, sidled round to the piano. Marianne turned, saw her and raced over to her.

' 'Arry. Where were you? Why didn't you come to class? I worried about you.'

'But, Marianne – I left a note at the stage door for you to tell you. Mme Dupont took me to do class at Studio Goncourt and—'

'I did not get a note. I thought – I thought you were angry or – or fed up or something. Maybe gone home even. I rang but no one answered and Sylvie never goes out in the morning.'

'Oh, Marianne, I'm sorry. No, of course I wouldn't go home. I'm here. But I missed doing class so much and we did leave a note, we did, down with the concierge . . .'

'I didn't stop there. I came in with Will and we were talking. I just thought – I was a bit worried – I mean, my mother can be – well . . .'

Harriet put a hand on her arm and then suddenly hugged her tight.

'No, it wasn't your mother. I didn't see her again. Only Mme Dupont.' She smiled and stepped back. 'She was so kind, Marianne, so kind . . . and I went to this brilliant, amazing class at—' She glanced at Alistair. 'I'll tell you about it later. Listen, I'm here now and I'm not going anywhere till you've done the pas de deux and everything's OK. Where's Will? Doing his hair I bet. What colour are the highlights today?'

Marianne relaxed and giggled. 'Bright purple – like a plum.'

Harriet gave a small, invisible sigh of relief and laughed with her. Alistair came over.

'We are going down on stage now, Marianne,' he said. 'Are you ready?' He turned to Harriet. 'If you come down, Harriet, you must sit in the stalls and not talk. As a rule I would say no one watching at all, but I know Marianne would like you to be there.'

Harriet nodded, a bit miffed that he should think she wouldn't know how to behave at a time like this, but she fell in behind them as they left the studio. The narrow stairs wound down through pools of light and shadow from bare bulbs on the landings. Watching Marianne's silhouette going down in front of her, Harriet frowned as she saw how horribly thin she was now. She seemed to stagger slightly, caught at the handrail and stopped. Alistair looked at her, his face full of concern.

'Marianne?'

'Sorry, Alistair. I just slipped. I was not thinking.'

Alistair nodded but said nothing. He walked ahead of Marianne down the stairs.

Harriet frowned. That was no slip. Marianne's knees had gone and if she hadn't held on she'd have fallen. All thoughts of the class at the Studio

Goncourt put away, she knew she must get Marianne to eat, or at least to talk about it, face the problem . . . maybe get her back to Mme Dupont . . . Or she could get Gareth on Will's mobile and ask him to try . . . But that meant telling Will and he had more than enough to cope with.

On stage, Will was already warming up, taking the width of the stage at a leap, pirouettes, entrechats, cabrioles and a sudden backflip into a flamboyant pose, coming out of it giggling into a deep flashy obeisance to the empty auditorium. Highlights aflame like a ripe Victoria under the harsh working light, he turned to them with grin.

'Might as well make the most of it while I'm here,' he said. 'Oop là! Now then, La Marianna, let's give it the full bezzaz? OK?'

Alistair laughed but put an arm round Will's shoulders. 'I think we'll take it a little easy to start with, Will. Let's do the lifts first. There's plenty of time. We're on stage till four if we need to be.'

They took it slowly, dissecting each of the lifts, adjusting to the rake of the stage. Harriet sat in the front row watching anxiously. Marianne was jumpy and a bit scratchy when things didn't go right first time, but Will kept his cool, Alistair was patient and they began to link longer phrases together.

'OK,' said Alistair, 'shall we have a go right through, then?'

Just as he leant over to speak to the pianist below him in the orchestra pit, there was a stir at the end of the row. Harriet looked across. Miss McGregor was standing there with Jessica. She whispered something to her, turned and went towards the doors at the back of the auditorium. Jessica made herself comfortable, tucking her feet up underneath her in the velvet armchair, leaning her cheek on one hand as she looked up at the stage, and, Harriet thought grimly, by the look on her face, already prepared for a good bitch. She wouldn't *do* anything now, even she wouldn't dare, but later she could cause mayhem. And if Marianne saw her suddenly when she wasn't expecting her . . .

She looked up at the stage. Marianne had her back to the audience, but she saw Will glance down and his expression change. He rolled his eyes at Harriet over Marianne's shoulder. Taking care to keep her turned away, with his hand on her back, he led Marianne to the corner, ready to start the pas de deux.

'Don't worry, people,' said Alistair, 'this'll be a kind of struggle-through. You're not used to the stage – there's the size and the rake to remember – but let's just see how it goes. Thank you, Roy.' He nodded down at the pianist, and the music began.

Harriet tried to relax but found herself holding her breath for the really difficult lifts. Things seemed to be going fairly well, however, until suddenly Marianne stopped.

'I can't hear the music,' she said.

'Will?' said Alistair.

'It's not great,' said Will. 'Is the stage relay on?'

Alistair sighed impatiently and strode into the wings where Mike Simms was standing with the French Stage Director. While they were talking, Will took care to keep Marianne's attention away from the auditorium. There was a slight crackle from high-up at the side of the stage and Alistair returned.

'Roy, can you give us a tinkle,' he said into the orchestra pit, and the pianist ran his fingers up and down the keyboard. The music came over loud and clear and Alistair turned, ready to start again . . . but the damage was done. Marianne had looked down at the pianist and caught sight of Jessica. Her face dropped. She turned to Will with a scowl, then turned to Alistair. She spoke to him quietly, but her shoulders were tense and her fingers drummed against her legs.

Alistair turned. 'Oh, Jessica, you're here,' he said. 'Who said you could—'

'Miss McGregor,' said Jessica in a voice that said 'even you can't argue with that'.

'I see. Well, I did ask for no one to be at this rehearsal,' said Alistair.

'But I *am* understudy,' said Jessica, chin in the air. Harriet drew in a shocked breath.

'Yes, I know, but even so . . .' said Alistair. 'You'll get a quick chance tomorrow. I'm sorry, Jessica, that's all there's time for. We need this rehearsal to ourselves.'

Jessica stood up with a noisy sigh, letting the seat bang upwards. Hand on hip, she gave a pointed glance towards Harriet.

'Look,' said Alistair, holding up his hands, 'OK, there's no time to argue, but just keep very quiet, will you? You know how difficult this is, Jessica, so . . .'

'Of course,' she said.

Alistair gave a curt nod and turned back to Marianne and Will. With a quiet smirk to herself and a glance at Harriet from the corner of her eye, Jessica sat down and resumed her pose. Harriet looked up at Marianne anxiously, but Will had his hand firmly on Marianne's shoulder, had turned her away from the auditorium and was leading her up to the corner to start the pas de deux. Alistair stepped to the front of the stage and turned to watch them. At the piano, Roy ran his hands over the keys again and the music came clearly over the tannoy. The dance started, Alistair moving with them, slowing down and speeding up with them, his eyes never leaving them, speaking quietly: 'That's it . . . stretch and turn and – no, no, drop the arm – yes, beautiful . . .'

Suddenly, Harriet sat bolt upright. Marianne! What was happening to Marianne? She seemed to be – somehow, disappearing, coming and going, lost in a kind of mist. A figure stood in the shadows, just visible in the wings, white hands stretched towards Marianne. Harriet ran her hand over her eyes and glanced along at Jessica – but she was still curled up in the seat, unperturbed. Harriet looked back. The figure was still there, reaching out to Marianne. She was all in white, a drift of leaves down the front of her dress. Giuseppina . . . It must be Giuseppina, but what . . . ? And then the music – over the tannoy the piano faded and the *Coppélia* music seemed to leak through, blaring out. Harriet put her hands over her ears. How could Marianne not hear it – not be aware of what was happening?

Suddenly, the stage darkened and, in a single spotlight, the figure in white ran a dancer's run to the centre of the stage and looked straight at Harriet, great dark eyes seeming to implore her to listen. Harriet dropped her hands and Giuseppina spoke . . . But it was too far away and in French and Harriet couldn't understand. With a little cry, Giuseppina whirled and ran towards Marianne. Harriet jumped up and shouted: 'Marianne – look out!'

The figure vanished and the music stopped. The pas de deux ground to a halt and Alistair looked round, glaring.

'What on earth – Harriet! What are you doing? Be quiet! You could have—'

'I – I'm sorry – I thought – I mean . . . Didn't you see – hear the . . . ?'

Marianne and Will came to the front of the stage and looked over.

'What's the matter, Harry?' said Will. 'Was there something wrong . . . ?' He glanced along at Jessica who was sitting bolt upright in her chair.

'No,' said Harriet. 'I'm sorry – I thought – I thought . . .'

Will shrugged, looking puzzled and annoyed, but quickly drew Marianne back centre stage and started persuading her to go over some steps. She looked shaken and tried to push him away. With an angry glance back at Harriet, he persevered and gradually began to calm Marianne, but Alistair angrily slapped a hand against his side.

'That's it. I've had enough. Everybody out of the auditorium. Go on, Harriet, please go. You too, Jessica. There's been nothing but trouble with this piece and I'm not putting up with it any more. Go on, off you go, both of you. You're lucky there wasn't an accident,' he added, glowering at Harriet as she shifted along the row towards the door, almost in tears.

He was right. She was no better than Jessica. She looked up at Will and Marianne, trying to catch an eye to let them know how distressed she was, how sorry that she had upset everything, but they were absorbed again now and didn't see her. But Will, she felt, was deliberately keeping his back to her.

As she left, she heard Alistair say irritably, 'I said, you too, Jessica. Go *on*. I'll see you with Will tomorrow – if we get that far.' As she went through the pass-door and down the passageway at the side of the stage, Harriet sensed rather than saw Jessica follow her out. She didn't want to speak to her, but nor did she want her to think she was afraid of her. She slipped through the double doors on to the stage itself and flattened herself against the wall in case Jessica had noticed her escape, but Jessica's footsteps padded past into the distance. Harriet slumped silently on to the floor, her head on her knees.

She sat there for what seemed an age, not moving, hardly breathing, until she heard the rehearsal draw to a close. From the voices on stage, it hadn't ended well; Will was still making placatory noises but Marianne sounded strident and anxious.

Harriet scrambled quietly to her feet, ready to dodge out of the door before anyone could see her, when a sudden draught whipped past her, catching her breath. She shivered and started to push through the doors but a voice through the tannoy stopped her. ' 'Arriette . . . 'Arriette,' it said in a whisper.

She paused and turned. Someone speaking to her through the tannoy? It couldn't be. She listened. More crackles and then the voice came again, urgent, pleading: 'Dis-lui . . . je t'en prie . . . dis-lui que—' but there was a shout from Alistair to a technician and, with a fizz and a click, the tannoy cut out.

She hurried out of the door and stopped. That voice had said ' 'Arriette'. French. But French with a strange accent. Talking to her. It can't have been Marianne; Marianne was with Will and Alistair still. A techie? She had seen women technicians around, but they didn't know her and why should they speak to her?

Giuseppina. Giuseppina had tried to speak to her before, on the stage, when she thought she was running at Marianne. But would Giuseppina know about tannoys? And 'dis-lui que . . .' – what did that mean? Totally bewildered, she ran her hands over her head and clasped them behind her neck, her elbows tight together in front of her, gazing down at the steps ahead, seeking an answer. What was happening to her? To Marianne? To them all?

Suddenly a voice barked her name and she whirled round. Miss McGregor stood in the passage, her arms folded, her jaw set, her eyes furious.

'There you are, Harriet. I've been looking for you everywhere since that disgraceful exhibition in the auditorium. Where have you been?'

'I – I . . .'

'It doesn't matter. What matters is that you don't go to any more rehearsals from now on. And you will not be in the wings for the performance either.' She jabbed a pointed fingernail on the metal stair rail in time with her words: 'I will not tolerate such behaviour in any student.'

'Oh, please . . .'

'No, Harriet. I won't have it. Alistair was right. You could have caused a serious accident. Marianne is not dancing well as it is. I daresay your presence isn't helping. I was against your coming in the first place.'

'It's not *me* . . .' burst out Harriet. 'Honestly, it isn't me that's the—'

'That will do!' Miss McGregor almost screamed with rage. She paused to recover herself, her nostrils distended as she controlled her breathing. She closed her eyes briefly, then, gripping the handrail, her knuckles showing white, she looked at Harriet, icy calm.

'That will do, Harriet. Blaming other people is *not* going to help you. You were out of order in that rehearsal and you know you were. Don't make excuses and don't blame other people. Now . . .'

Harriet held on to what little courage she had left. 'Please, Miss McGregor. I'm really, really sorry. I was just startled by something that – I thought there was going to be an accident and—'

'Now you are lying, Harriet. I was at the back of the auditorium throughout the rehearsal. Nothing happened to startle you or anyone. I was there. I would have seen it.'

Harriet shook her head in despair. What could she say? She tried one last time.

'All right, Miss McGregor, I'll go. I'm sorry. I didn't mean . . .' She looked up. 'But, please, could you – there's just one thing – I . . .'

'Oh, come on, Harriet, out with it. I've wasted enough time on this as it is. I've other more important things to do.'

'Yes, I know. Please, please . . .' and out it came with a rush . . . 'please don't let Jessica into rehearsal either – Marianne is—'

'That's enough. Jessica is understudy and will be at rehearsals when required. At the rate Marianne is going, Jessica will—' She cut herself off abruptly. 'I don't want to discuss this any longer. Harriet, you will wait for Marianne at the stage door. You will not go to the dressing-room and you will not return tomorrow. You may of course see Marianne out of rehearsal time, I can't stop you, but may I make it quite clear that you are not welcome in the theatre while we are here. Do you understand?'

Harriet felt tears well up. She closed her eyes and her head dropped.

'Yes, Miss McGregor.' She was barely audible.

'Your petty jealousies and squabbles with Jessica have no place here. Now go and wait by the stage door for Marianne. I will tell her where you are.'

Unable to speak for the lump of misery stuck in her throat, Harriet nodded. She hurried down the stairs, her rucksack hugged to her, and away down the shadowy hallway to the stage door, where the television was still burbling away in the concierge's room.

What a mess she had made of everything. She hadn't done anything she'd set out to do. Only Will was keeping Jessica and Marianne apart. Marianne still wasn't eating. The pas de deux wasn't going well and now she'd made things worse.

She stepped through the stage door and leant against the grimy wall outside, too dejected to cry. What would Marianne say when she came out? What would Will say? She'd let him down worse than anyone in a way. Why had she come to Paris at all? She wanted to forget it all, and run away home.

# Chapter 12

Harriet hardly raised her head as Miss Esbester stepped out of the stage door, ducking through the low entrance as she came.

'Harriet? What's all this I hear? What have you been doing?' Miss Esbester's voice was brisk but her eyes looked sympathetic. With an effort, Harriet pushed herself away from the wall and hoiked her rucksack on to her shoulder. She heaved a sigh.

'I've made a mess of everything, that's what,' she said. 'I – I'm really, really sorry. I tried to say to Miss McGregor but . . .'

'What happened exactly?'

Harriet shrugged. How could she explain without Miss Esbester thinking her out of her mind – seeing dead dancers rushing about on the stage?

'I – I thought there was going to be an – an accident – a kind of collision . . . and I jumped up and called out. It was such a stupid thing to do.'

'I know you wouldn't have done it deliberately, Harriet. It must have been something quite urgent that made you react the way you did?'

This wasn't quite a direct question, so Harriet licked her lips and gave a kind of half-nod. Miss Esbester carried on.

'Well, never mind now. The main thing is, you're worried about Marianne, aren't you?'

Harriet nodded. She looked up at the lined face with its beaky nose. Everyone said that Miss Esbester would probably be retiring soon, and Harriet thought that was sad. She was a good teacher and had always been very kind to her.

'Well,' said Miss Esbester, 'there's not much I can do for the moment. Things are . . .' she gave a little smile '. . . things are a bit *hot-house* in there, if you know what I mean. It's best left to cool off for the moment. But what about Marianne? Is it Jessica that's the problem?'

Harriet hesitated. Should she tell this nice woman everything? It would take a huge weight from her own shoulders, but what if it meant Marianne couldn't dance at the matinée? And she recognized with a little stab that it wasn't just Marianne getting into trouble that worried her; part of it was not wanting Jessica to dance in her place.

Jessica didn't deserve it and she wasn't any good, not in the pas de deux – in other things maybe, but not in that.

She suddenly made a decision. She would talk to Mme Dupont tonight about the eating. She would deal with the Jessica problem now.

'They – they don't get on.'

'I think we all realize that, Harriet. It's pretty obvious. But these things happen, you know, especially in a school like this or even in a company. Dancers have to deal with it.'

'I know. I do know. And usually Marianne can take care of herself. It can be almost – almost funny, sometimes. But right now . . .'

'Yes, I understand.'

'Will's being really brilliant. He's with Marianne all the time when I can't be, just so there isn't any trouble. He knows what Jessica's like and, well . . . and Marianne too when she feels like it.'

'You can't keep them apart all the time, Harriet.'

'No, no, of course not. But Marianne shouldn't have to waste time and – and energy fighting back someone who's just plain jealous. And usually it wouldn't affect her dancing, but now, with the performance coming on and Gareth being injured like that and Marianne getting used to Will and –

and oh, just everything . . .' She gave her rucksack a thump against the wall.

Miss Esbester put a hand on her shoulder. 'Now then, Harriet, this isn't like you. Stop panicking. Marianne is tougher than you think.'

Harriet avoided her eyes. 'Is she?'

Miss Esbester smiled. 'I think so. I know she certainly takes Jessica on when she needs to. Just the same, I do understand that this is a difficult time for her and her performance mustn't suffer. She's going to be upset about what's happened to you.'

'I've made things worse. Much worse, haven't I?'

'Well . . . maybe. But – I do agree that we have to do some damage limitation.' She gave another little smile. 'So I'll see what I can do.'

'Will you – will you really?' Harriet looked up eagerly.

'I can't promise, but I'll try.' Miss Esbester smiled again with a little nod. Harriet had trouble not flinging her arms round her. 'First I'll have a word with Marianne, before she leaves. I'll explain you acted for the – shall we say, best of motives.'

She paused. Harriet couldn't bring herself to respond to this hint to tell the kindly teacher why she had leapt up like that. She simply said a heartfelt

161

'Thank you' instead. Miss Esbester's eyebrows flickered but she continued.

'Seriously, Harriet. I can't promise anything. Miss McGregor is in charge of this performance and what she says goes. You understand? But I will try. At the very least, things might not be so bad when we get back. People will have calmed down by then anyway. Now, cheer up and don't be miserable when Marianne comes out. That's not what she needs now.'

With a final pat of Harriet's arm, Miss Esbester went back into the theatre, leaving Harriet in a turmoil. Miss Esbester was one of the few teachers who really listened and she hadn't asked probing questions as most of the others would . . . But – but . . . it was best not to bank on being allowed back in to watch rehearsals, that was certain. And what was she going to say to Marianne about what had happened that afternoon? And what *was* she going to do about making Marianne eat? Should she have said anything about that to Miss Esbester? So many questions battering her.

Marianne would be a while if Miss Esbester was going back to talk to her. Harriet walked a little way up the street, passing the old man pottering with the little dog still patrolling the lampposts. Ordinarily she would have bent down to give the dog a pat, but not now . . . She concentrated on how to explain to Marianne and Will why she had disrupted the rehearsal like that. But how could she explain Giuseppina? Will was certainly not going to believe that story. Yet something in her knew that she must find the link between the little ballerina and Marianne, and suddenly, looking up at the back of the great Opéra building, she thought of a way she just might find it. She needed to know more about Giuseppina. She needed to know her story.

The archive. Where was the archive? Not through the stage door, she was pretty certain. It must be through the front entrance. She turned to walk back, stepping aside to avoid a woman loaded with shopping. As she did so, something caught her eye across the street.

Someone was standing there, someone that seemed somehow familiar. Harriet stared. At the near end of a dark, gloomy passage leading away from the far pavement stood a girl. She had her back to Harriet. Dark ringlets hung down over the collar of a shabby dark red coat, tight-fitting with a tiny waist. Her feet in their cracked leather ankle-boots were turned out. Between the boots and the coat was a small expanse of black-stockinged leg, a large darn just visible. On her head perched a little hat with a moth-eaten feather.

'Giuseppina!'

Harriet kept her voice low. She didn't want to frighten her, nor did she want to draw attention to them both. But she wanted the answers to a lot of questions. Urgently, and without looking, she stepped out to cross the road and an angry van driver tooted at her. She dodged away with an impatient wave of her hand. When she reached the other side, the girl was moving slowly away from her down the passage.

Short, narrow and foul, the passage ended in a grimy stone wall with a patch of green slime reaching up from the ground. Filthy, cracked windows fronted two empty shops on one side. In one, a ragged curtain hung festooned abjectly in ribbons, trailing cobwebs. Outside lay a pile of rotting rubbish. On the other side were small crumbling houses, evil-looking, oozing damp. From a rusting wrought-iron support, a single ancient gas lamp hung crookedly from a wall and overhead the remains of a couple of wrought-iron girders supported a few broken panes of glass. Harriet drew back with a grimace, feeling a chill run down her spine. What a horrible place.

Ahead of her, the girl seemed to stagger, putting out a hand to a wall then righting herself, not wanting to touch it. She turned.

Yes, it was Giuseppina, but a Giuseppina gaunt and grey, quite unlike the beautiful, shy young ballerina she had been in the photograph and when Harriet had seen her run across the stage. Her eyes were sunk back in her head and her cheeks were hollow. With a worried frown, Harriet ventured a little way towards her, but the reek of decay made her stop and put her hand over her mouth. She took a deep breath through her fingers and called again, her voice little more than a whisper.

'Giuseppina, I know it's you. Please – please tell me. What's happened to you? What do you want? What are you trying to tell me?'

The little dancer raised her arm slowly, the hand covered in a tight glove once white, now faded yellow. She beckoned. Harriet took a few steps further into the dank, festering passage. Icy cold now, she hesitated. This was a terrible place. What was Giuseppina doing here?

'Please,' she said, 'please tell me what you want. Why are you trying to speak to me? In the rehearsal – before – why did you run at Marianne like that?'

Giuseppina put her gloved hand to her lips. Her

dark eyes glowed huge in the dim light of the passage. She reached forward a little.

'Dis-lui,' came the whisper, 'dis-lui que . . .' and then a spate of French came so quickly and with such a heavy accent that Harriet shook her head in frustration, digging both fists into her cheeks hard and hissing out her words through clenched teeth.

'I don't understand. I don't understand you, Giuseppina. Go slowly, ple-e-ase.'

But Giuseppina shook her head. Her eyes seemed to burn, growing larger and larger, till tears ran down her pale cheeks.

'Dis-lui . . .' she said, but her voice, already low, faltered and died. She closed her eyes and seemed to draw away. Harriet went to take a step forward to follow her when she heard her name called behind her.

' 'Arriette!'

Harriet swung round. That was Marianne! Quickly! She must speak to Giuseppina, try one last time to understand her before Marianne reached them. But when she turned back, Giuseppina had vanished and the passage was nowhere to be seen. She was standing on the pavement outside a perfectly ordinary apartment block.

As Harriet stared up and down the street,

confused, Marianne crossed the road and grabbed her arm. Behind her was Will, his purple highlights bright but his face far from glowing as he stumped over towards Harriet.

'Over to you, *duckie*,' he said in his grittiest voice. 'I've had enough for one fun-packed day.' He planted a perfunctory kiss on Marianne's cheek. 'À demain,' he said, 'I *suppose*...' and he swept off, taking irritable little jumpy, skippy steps every now and again to hurry him away the quicker, the bag over his shoulder bumping up and down on his bottom indignantly as he went.

Marianne stood, her eyes dark with anger, looking first at the fast disappearing Will, then at Harriet. ' 'E is very angry with you, 'Arry. And me too. I am angry with you. You were supposed to be 'elping, not – not ... that was so bad, in the rehearsal. What were you thinking of? 'Ow could you ... ?'

Harriet shook her head and opened her mouth to try to answer but Marianne cut in. 'Now Miss McGregor say you cannot come into the theatre. Miss Esbester tried to tell me but I don't understand? Will and me, we were doing so well and now ... Why did you scream out like that?'

Harriet heaved a great sigh and closed her eyes.

'I don't know, Marianne,' she said, clutching the

back of her neck with one hand, trying to ease the muscles. 'It – it just happened – I just . . .'

'But, 'Arry . . .'

'Look . . . let's go home – I mean let's go to your mother's and I'll try and explain when I've sorted everything out for myself. There's a lot I don't understand, either.'

'But, 'Arry, you nearly ruined the rehearsal. Alistair was furious. And after that nothing go right – nothing.'

'I'm sorry, Marianne, really I am. Look, I'll—'

But a sudden call from up the street broke in.

'Marianne, ma petite! 'Arry! J'arrive – I am 'ere!' Mme Dupont was hurrying towards them. Marianne whirled round away from Harriet and flung herself at the dumpy little woman, almost knocking her sideways and sending kirbigrips scattering.

'Oh là, qu'est-ce que c'est, alors?' And a flood of French followed. Marianne burst into tears. Over her head, Mme Dupont looked at Harriet in alarm. Harriet could do nothing but shrug in despair.

'Come,' said Mme Dupont, patting Marianne gently. 'Allons-y. Let us go. We will – 'ow do you say . . . be sorting all this out at 'ome . . .'

Marianne drew back quickly, pushing the hair out of her eyes. 'Is my mother there?'

'Non, chérie, there was a matinée. She is at zer théatre. She will stay till after the spectacle – the show.'

Marianne nodded, rubbing a hand over her eyes. She looked at Harriet, tears still streaking her face. ' 'Arry, that was very bad today. You should not 'ave done that but . . .'

Again Mme Dupont looked at Harriet in alarm. Harriet held up her hands and shook her head. 'It was – it was – I can't explain here. But I will, Marianne, I will.'

Marianne shook her head, still unconvinced, Harriet was sure, but she no longer looked quite so angry.

'There's so much I need to know . . .' said Harriet. 'Would it be all right if – well, there is something I need to do first before I come back.'

Marianne went to protest but Mme Dupont broke in quickly.

'Bien sûr, ma petite. Whatever you want. Marianne and me, we will go 'ome and 'ave a nice tisane. Tisane make everyt'ing calm, alors, hein? Do you know the way back, 'Arriette?'

'Yes, I think so. Yes, I do. I'll be fine. I'm just going back into the theatre for a while. I won't be long, Marianne, I promise. Then we'll sort it out.'

'But you are not allowed . . .' said Marianne.

'It'll be all right where I'm going. It's not backstage so I don't see how anyone will know.'

Marianne frowned. 'Why – what are you going to do – 'Arry, I don't like—'

Harriet went to her and put her arms round her. She was stiff, unyielding, but Harriet just kept hugging her till she relaxed a little. 'I'm truly, truly sorry about what happened. I will explain everything when I come back, Marianne, honestly, I promise. Just go home with Mme Dupont and I'll come as soon as I can.'

Mme Dupont took Marianne by the arm and they went off up the street, Marianne glancing back half-anxious, still half-angry, over her shoulder. Harriet waved them off and waited till they had gone. Then she went round to the front of the theatre, took a deep breath and started up the steps.

# Chapter 13

The young man in the archive couldn't have been nicer. He looked at Harriet over his horn-rimmed spectacles and said, 'Giuseppina Bozzacchi, hmm, let me see now. I don't think I have ever been asked about her before but . . . I know who you mean . . .'

He prodded his computer, staring into it with fierce concentration, and then went off on long gangling legs to hunt along one of the endless shelves lining the bright, spacious room. Harriet gazed round her. The light from the huge windows, the pink marble columns and the white-painted wood panelling covered in huge photographs of dancers in 1930s costumes gave it an almost partyish feel. The women in the photographs had Cupid's bow lips and lots of beads on their tutus. The men had boot-polish hair and rather wrinkly-looking tights. But Harriet wasn't thinking of parties, just of Giuseppina in that filthy, stinking passage, her eyes filled with tears –

and of Marianne's angry, tear-stained face too.

The librarian returned with a large book and the book of photographs that Harriet already had. 'This is all I can find, I'm afraid,' he said in his perfect English. 'There's not much about her it would seem. But there should be something in here.'

He settled Harriet at a table by the window and she glanced down into the great square below, the Place de l'Opéra, busy with people bustling up and down the steps of the Métro, others settling at the tables under the bright umbrellas of the restaurants lining the square.

'We shall be closing quite soon, mademoiselle,' said the librarian, 'but as there is so little information, I think you will be all right.'

'Thank you,' said Harriet. 'Oh!' she burst out, suddenly anxious. 'I don't speak French, well – only a few words, and I can't really read it at all.'

'Don't worry. The book is in English. It is by one of your great ballet historians. He has done a great deal of work on the late nineteenth century, but it is a period not much studied here. We have the archive, of course, but people mostly ask for information on very early dance, the Romantics of course, like Marie Taglioni, or the early twentieth century.'

Harriet flicked over the pages of pictures in the

book she knew, left it open at Giuseppina's photograph and propped it up in front of her. 'All right, Giuseppina,' she muttered very quietly, 'let's see what your secrets are. Let's see what this is all about.'

She opened the second book. For a moment she didn't know where to start but then, with a sigh of exasperation at her stupidity, she turned to the index. There was just one entry for Bozzacchi and only a couple of paragraphs at that.

The first told Harriet nothing she didn't know already. A little bit about the ballet *Coppélia*, the choreographer, the composer, how Giuseppina Bozzacchi had been the first ballerina to dance Swanilda and the date, 1869. Harriet glanced up at Giuseppina in the other book leaning on the windowsill in front of her. There she stood in her white tulle. Harriet smiled at the small face looking out at her so seriously, gave her a little nod and returned to her reading. But as the book went on to unfold Giuseppina's tragic tale, her face grew serious.

The very first dancer chosen as Swanilda was the prima ballerina of the Opéra, but she had been taken ill, and was too ill to dance for a long while. The ballet master and the choreographer searched and searched for the right replacement and finally found

Giuseppina, a young Italian girl, among the Petits Rats, the students at the Opéra. They spent weeks grooming her for the role. Italian! Of course, she was Italian! That accounted for the accent.

*Coppélia* was instantly a huge success. Giuseppina, with her dark, flashing eyes and exuberant smile, had taken Paris by storm. Her brilliant technique had made audiences gasp. She had given only eighteen performances, but it was enough to bring the whole city to her feet. But within days, war was declared, the Prussians invaded France and the siege of Paris began. The city was surrounded with guns and cannon and the people began to starve. The Opéra closed and Giuseppina danced no more. Poverty-stricken, she hid with her mother and her young sister in the place where she lived, a gloomy passage not far from the Opéra itself . . .

Harriet looked up. 'Is that where I saw you?' she whispered. 'Is that terrible place where you lived?' She turned the page. A photograph seemed to leap out at her, a photograph of the passage she had seen, squalid buildings, broken arcade roof, piles of rubbish. 'Passage Saulnier,' she read, 'where Giuseppina Bozzacchi lived and died.'

'Oh, Giuseppina,' breathed Harriet, 'no wonder you looked so ill . . .'

There was little more to read. Towards the end of the siege, cholera spread like wildfire through Paris. Giuseppina, destitute and hungry, caught the terrible disease. Within a few days, she was dead. She died on the morning of her seventeenth birthday, in November 1870, alone with her mother and sister, forgotten by the Paris crowds, and neglected ever since.

Harriet dropped her head into her hands. Poor, beautiful, talented Giuseppina, working so hard to succeed, dancing with such fire, such life, lighting up the stage for such a little while . . . such a little while.

She looked at the photograph. 'It's a horrible story. But it isn't a story, it's true. I can't bear it . . .'

She sat for a moment, not wanting to move. She thought of Swanilda, the playful, quick-witted heroine of *Coppélia*, teasing, imperious. How those dark eyes in the photograph must have shone with mischief as Giuseppina spun and leapt and sped across the stage, winding the keys that made the dolls dance, jerking like puppets – the wizard, the Chinese mandarin, the kilted Scottish doll – upsetting Doctor Coppelius, making her friends giggle. Then that last pas de deux with the penitent Franz, tender and lyrical, but full of difficult, elegant steps that needed such confidence and skill. And then the obeisance, the deep curtsey, the wild applause of the adoring crowds, the flowers falling at her feet as she knelt in her white tulle . . . And the sad, sunken eyes closing at last in that terrible place, forgotten, starving and in pain.

At last Harriet closed the books and stood up. 'I'm glad I know your story,' she said quietly, 'but Giuseppina, poor Giuseppina, I don't see how it answers my questions . . . what this has to do with Marianne. And why you are trying to speak to me . . . what it is you want to say.'

Sadly, she took the books back to the desk where the young man sat. He was talking into the phone with great animation, nodding emphatically, stabbing the air with a finger, his brow furrowed. Harriet stood a little way from the desk, still thinking about the brilliant young ballerina, not wanting to intrude on his conversation.

'Non, non, non,' he said. Suddenly something he said made her whip round towards him. 'Dis-lui . . .' he was saying 'dis-lui que . . .' and the rest was lost in a flow of French.

'Dis-lui que' – that's what Giuseppina had said, over the tannoy and again in the passage. 'Dis-lui que . . .'

The librarian put down the phone and looked up. 'Finished already?' he said, with a smile. 'Did you find what you want?'

'Yes . . . yes, thank you,' said Harriet. 'Well, there wasn't much, like you said, but – but – it was such a sad story . . . She died, very young, of some terrible disease, just when she was . . . um . . . sorry – excuse me, but could I ask you a question?'

'You can try. But I don't know much about Second Empire dancers.'

'It isn't that,' said Harriet, wondering if she had the nerve to ask him something about his own phone conversation. 'It's – well, you know I told you I don't speak French . . . well, I heard someone say something I didn't understand, and you said the very same thing when you were on the phone – and I wondered what it meant. Dee looee – something like that . . .'

'Dis-lui? Oh, that means "tell him" – it would be something like "dis-lui que" – and then what you want him to be told, if you see what I mean. "Tell him that" – oh I don't know – "dis-lui que je veux le voir à six heures – tell him that I'd like to meet him at six o'clock". Something like that.'

'Oh, I see,' said Harriet. 'I see . . . yes, I'm not sure it makes sense but – thank you.' She was supposed to tell someone something – a man, a boy . . . but who and what?

'Thank you very much,' she said, frowning a little, still puzzled. 'I hope I haven't kept you late.'

'No, no,' said the young man, 'it was a pleasure. And I think I'll have a look at Giuseppina Bozzacchi – it sounds a very interesting story.'

'It is,' said Harriet, deep in thought. As she opened the door, the librarian stood up, leant over the desk and called after her: 'Of course it can mean "tell her", as well.'

Harriet swung round and met his eyes behind the big glasses. He gave an enthusiastic little nod. 'Dislui,' he said, 'what you were asking . . . it can mean "tell her", as well as "tell him".'

'Oh, oh I see,' said Harriet. 'Tell *her* . . . I see . . . thank you.'

She padded down the carpet on the wide staircase, the brass fittings twinkling in the evening sun just peering through a fanlight far above; then on she went through the darkened hall, where the great chandelier hung waiting to light up for the evening performance, waiting for the crowds of glittering people to come in and banish the shadows.

'Tell her . . . tell her . . .'

She pushed out through the ornate glass doors and

stood on the top step, blinking slightly at the sudden light. But the sun dipped behind a cloud and Harriet shivered. It seemed very quiet, the great square suddenly almost empty. She put out a foot to go down the stairs and met the pavement – except that the big flagstones had disappeared and she was standing on cobblestones. She looked down, startled, then up again and all around her, slowly at first, then spinning to face each side of the square, faster, faster.

Where had the steps gone? Where was she? Where was the Métro? Where was the Grand Boulevard leading to the Galeries? Where were the cafés, the umbrellas – the people . . . She stopped, steadying herself, hanging on to her rucksack, the only familiar thing she could find. Even the buildings round about were different: shorter, narrower, closer together. The square itself seemed to have shrunk. She looked behind her. The Opéra had vanished. In its place was a smaller, much lower building, with a colonnade down the side. A few people, thin and tattered like scarecrows, were huddled against the columns, heads bowed in misery or lying on the cold stones, no more than a heap of filthy rags. Others peered around them with desperate eyes, rat-like and predatory, fingers scrabbling at their torn clothes, their hair thin and wild.

One or two of the scarecrow people started to crawl towards her . . . holding out hands like claws towards her, closer, closer . . . Hastily, she backed away into the open. One of them caught her eye and struggled nearer. She stepped back quickly, shaking her head involuntarily. He stopped, staring at her, but finally dropped his gaze, and slowly, one at a time, they melted back into the shadows of the colonnade. She turned, and with a glance or two behind her to make sure they weren't following, went a little further across the square and stopped to get her bearings. There was nothing round her that she recognized. She was lost.

Feeling vulnerable out in the open, she made for a corner where a few people were gathered. They seemed less threatening than the people under the colonnade, standing patiently, their backs towards her. Perhaps she could ask them the way, make them understand somehow . . .

But as she neared them she stopped. These people seemed to be waiting for something. They stood quietly, some clutching at others, almost too weak to stand, not menacing like the scarecrow people, but still gaunt, sick and suffering. Their clothes were worn out but at least were recognizably clothes. She took a step nearer. They were dressed like

Giuseppina had been in the passage: little boots, cracked and down-at-heel; tiny hats, their feathers gone; once tight-waisted coats hanging loose and frayed. The men's trousers drooped slack and shapeless, their jackets grimy and threadbare. How thin they all looked, how pale . . .

Suddenly, the people began to peer away to the right, some staggering to keep on their feet, gazing up a narrow street leading into the square. Harriet watched aghast as a small procession drew near. Four grey, shrunken men shuffled towards her bearing a coffin on their shoulders. The coffin had been knocked together out of cheap, splintered wood. It was small, yet the men's backs were bent almost double with exhaustion. As they approached, Harriet saw on the coffin a single bedraggled flower that slipped and slid across the lid. Behind the coffin came a young girl, no more than twelve years old, her ringlets matted and straggling over her shoulders, her face white and drawn. She wept as if she would never stop, clutching the hand of a woman in a worn, stained black dress; but the woman's hand was slack and her huge eyes dry, glazed over with despair. She looked too ill, too desperate to cry.

Harriet stood very still as they passed. The people watching bowed their heads and for some it was too much effort to raise them again. Harriet closed her eyes. She knew who was in the coffin. She knew whose funeral this was. She raised her head and waited, somehow certain that something more would happen.

The wan little figure of the young girl came past her, hesitated and turned back. The big dark eyes were soft and wide, the image of Giuseppina's. The white cheeks were wet with tears. Giuseppina's sister. She looked at Harriet, letting go her mother's hand, and her mother trudged on, unaware that she had left her. Slowly, the girl raised her hand towards the coffin as it lurched away on the shoulders of the exhausted men. She looked at Harriet.

'Giuseppina.' Harriet managed just one word.

The girl gave the vestige of a nod. She took a step towards Harriet, gathered her strength and raised her hands. She passed them to and fro in front of her, shaking her head – a ballet gesture. Harriet fought to remember. What did it mean? Yes, yes, that was it – *'no'*, *'must not'*, *'don't want'* – what did this girl not want?

Again the hands were lifted, light as if the wind had blown them. They revolved slowly round each other . . . *'Dance, dancer,'* whispered Harriet. The girl looked at her, her eyes even larger and deeper as she nodded again just once. Slowly, with huge effort, she lifted her hands a third time, this time in fists above her head and brought them down in front of her, one above the other. Gently, and so, so sadly, she lowered her head.

'*Death.*' That gesture meant death.

The girl placed her hands together in a gesture of prayer, holding them out towards Harriet . . . and suddenly she was gone.

' "*Asking*" – asking me for what . . . ?'

Harriet pressed her face between her hands, thinking urgently. What did it mean? She knew Giuseppina's story already. She knew how she had died – why tell it all over again in this strange, terrifying way?

She looked round her and blinked in a sudden light. On either side of her, people hurried across the Place de l'Opéra. The Métro belched another spate of travellers out into the early evening sunshine. She looked behind her. The Opéra itself was beginning to come to life. The chandelier was blazing and the doors swinging, smiling people passing in and out. And outside, under the umbrellas, life in the cafés was back to normal. Waiters in white aprons strolled around with loaded trays and customers toyed with tall glasses of wine, glistening oysters and plump, glossy olives.

Dazed and confused, she turned back. Everything had happened so quickly – one minute she had been in the Opéra archive, then out in what must have been the old square that was here long before the new Opéra was built. Now here she was back again as if nothing had happened. But Giuseppina's sister, and the little coffin . . . that she *had* seen, she was certain. As she turned, something on a paving stone caught her eye. She bent down and picked it up.

In her hand lay a single silk flower, once blushed with pink, now faded, limp and trampled. The kind of flower that might have been in the bouquet of a young ballerina, fêted by the Paris crowd . . . the flower that had lain on a small coffin as it lurched along. Harriet held it close. Suddenly, everything became clear.

'I think I know what it is you want, Giuseppina. I think I understand . . .' she whispered. 'Don't worry. You can rest . . . you can rest . . . I'll tell her. I'll tell her now . . .'

She stood up, slung her rucksack over her shoulder and, grasping the flower tightly, hurried away towards the Grand Boulevard. She knew exactly where she was going and what she had to say when she got there. No more trying not to upset her. No more shilly-shallying about what to do. She must see

Marianne at once. The time had come for some straight talking.

But when she reached the apartment, Marianne had gone.

Marianne so cross. The door had shut. Somee
struggling
but when she asked the question, Madame
had gone

# Chapter 14

Madame Dupont sat in the kitchen clutching a tissue, her hair straggling from its bun, her face creased up and blotched, her nose red.

'Oh, Madame Dupont, what's wrong?' Her own face troubled, Harriet put an arm round her plump, drooping shoulders. The old woman gave a shuddering sigh.

'C'est tout à fait ma faute . . . it is my fault . . . she get angry, so angry, chérie. Then she – she run off, 'Arriette. I could not stop 'er.'

'Marianne?'

Madame Dupont nodded. She buried her face in the tissue, gave a huge sniff and looked up again with watery eyes.

'I try to make 'er eat.' She glanced at Harriet. 'Maybe I was folle – stupide. I make 'er take off 'er big jumper. There was terrible row. Then Mlle Cantal, she come in by surprise – you know? I did not expect

186

'er. She shout and scream too.' She shuddered. 'But Marianne . . . it was 'orrible. La pauvre petite – 'er bones – 'er bones – you could see – 'Arriette, you are right to be . . .' and she shook her head, her cheeks wobbling, her eyes looking into the distance, big with the memory of how Marianne had looked beneath the thick sweater.

'Right to be worried about her?' said Harriet. 'Yes, I am. Even more now—' She cut herself off. There was not time to try to explain about Giuseppina. Anyway – how could you explain a ghost? She must find Marianne quickly.

Suddenly the door flung open and Mlle Cantal stalked in, her hair a brittle, crackling yellow cloud around her head, a hairbrush in her hand. She frowned as she saw Harriet but swept past her and bent over Mme Dupont. Furious, she let forth a stream of French, banging on the table with the brush handle. Mme Dupont half-turned towards her, trying to answer, but before she could open her mouth, Marianne's mother stood up and rounded on Harriet.

'And you – you are to blame too . . .'

'But – but why? I've only tried to—'

'You kept wanting her to eat, she said. On and on. Things she should *not* eat if she is to dance. Ridiculous. What do any of you know about it? Look

187

at you – you will never dance. Not like Marianne. She is doing what she has to do to be a great dancer. A great star. A dancer must be—'

Harriet felt a great rush of rage flush her neck and up into her cheeks. 'A dancer has to be fit, strong and healthy,' she said, blurting out the words through her fury. 'Not skin and bone with no strength. And Marianne is going to be really ill if she goes on like this. That's all I've done. Try to tell her. Try to help her.'

'Well "all you have done", as you call it, is make her upset and make her run away.'

'Run away?'

'Run away to get away from your nagging, you and Sylvie.'

Harriet faltered. 'But – but I've hardly said anything to her. I've been so careful – I've tried not to worry her – I was going to wait till after . . .'

'Wait? You can't have waited. She was already angry with you when she left, n'est-ce pas, Sylvie?' But before Mme Dupont could reply she whirled back to Harriet. '*And* you did something outrageous in rehearsal and you are forbidden the theatre. When she has this important performance. The only reason you are here is to give her support.' She slammed the hairbrush on to the table again. 'But you fuss her about food – you behave badly in the theatre and now she has run off. Very upset. I am not surprised.'

Harriet stared at her, worried but still angry. This woman seemed more anxious about Marianne being a star than seeing how ill she was.

'Isn't she at the hostel – with the others?' she said, but thinking, *Please, Marianne, please be at the hostel with Will . . .*

'I have just telephoned the hostel. She is not there. No one has seen her.'

Harriet turned to Mme Dupont, snatching up her sweatshirt. 'We must go and find her.'

With a final sniff, Mme Dupont stuffed the tissue into her pocket and hauled herself to her feet, suddenly determined. She lumbered out into the hall. Mlle Cantal hurried after her.

'Idiot!' she screamed. 'How do you think you will find her? God knows where she has gone.'

'We must try,' muttered Mme Dupont, struggling into a shapeless old cardigan and picking up her bag. 'You are right, chérie,' she said to Harriet. 'We cannot just sit 'ere . . .' and with a glance at Mlle Cantal '. . . shouting – one at the other.'

She opened the front door and gently shoved Harriet through in front of her. 'Do not worry, Mademoiselle, we will find Marianne for you and we will take care of 'er . . .' Then she said to herself, but loud enough for Mlle Cantal to hear, 'Someone needs to . . .'

She followed Harriet out and quietly shut the door behind her. After a second, Harriet heard a heavy thud as the hairbrush was hurled after them, crashing against the wood and tumbling to the floor.

Mme Dupont gave an impatient shake of her head. 'Tcchhh! She will get over it. In ten minute she will remember 'er show tonight and off she will go, sweet like sugar. Like always, she leave Marianne to me. She will forget about 'er, hein?' and she ushered Harriet down the stairs. Outside, past the concierge, she stopped.

'But she is right, 'Arriette. 'Ow do we know where she has gone?'

'Can you think of anywhere, anyone, she might go to?'

'À l'Opéra?'

Harriet glanced at her watch. 'There won't be anyone there now, not from school,' she said. 'We could try but I think she's more likely to go back to the hostel in the end. Unless – unless – does she have any friends in Paris?'

Mme Dupont shrugged. 'It is two years she does not live 'ere. She lose – um . . .'

'Lose touch?' Harriet nodded. That was so easy to do. Here in this Paris street with Mme Dupont and all the worry of Marianne, Sheffield seemed a long, long way away. 'We could call in at the theatre on the way to the hostel,' she said, 'but I still think that's where she'll go.'

'Mademoiselle telephone to the 'ostel . . .'

'She'll still go back there. She'll have to. There's nowhere else.'

They hurried through the darkening streets, glancing into shops and cafés on the way. *Though a café is the last place she'd be*, thought Harriet. At the theatre, the concierge hardly shifted his eyes from the television to say he hadn't seen any of 'les Anglais' for some time. Grudgingly, he put out a call over the tannoy, but someone answered to say no one from the English school was in the building.

'Let's just go to the hostel,' said Harriet. 'At least Will should be there. He may know something.' Her heart sank as she remembered Will's angry back as he had gone up the street earlier on.

On the steps of the hostel, she hesitated. 'I – I think maybe it would be better if you went in and asked,' she said, dropping her eyes.

Mme Dupont looked at her. 'It is true, you cannot go into the theatre now?'

Harriet gave an abject little nod.

'Eh alors! What 'appen?'

'Doesn't matter now. I'll tell you when we've found Marianne. But I think it would be best for you to go and ask for her here. The teachers may be about. They'll think I – oh, I don't know . . .' She turned away abruptly, furious with herself, tears of anxiety about Marianne starting into her eyes. Mme Dupont nodded, pursing her lips, and stumped up the steps.

After what seemed like hours, she came out again, Will following her.

'She is there,' said Mme Dupont, a big smile on her face. 'She is asleep.'

'Oooh – thank – thank goodness,' said Harriet, clutching her head between her hands, her shoulders round her ears. She let out a big breath and looked at Will, who appeared, she was relieved to see, fairly friendly. 'Is she – is she all right?'

'It depends what you mean by all right, Harriet *dear*. She was in a right old state when she came in, I can tell you . . .' He eyed her and his mouth twitched. 'But half an hour's heart-to-heart avec moi and a quick telephonette to Gareth seemed to calm her down a bit.'

'Oh, Will. You're brilliant.' He pulled a face that said *I know, but I'm too modest to say so*, and Harriet smiled for the first time for hours. 'Phoning Gareth was a brilliant idea. Is he OK?'

Will shrugged. 'I only said "hello" and passed him on to Marianne. After that I did the tactful hero bit – slid lightly out of the room like a *silver* shadow.' He flung an imaginary cape around him and tiptoed down the steps, his eyes sparkling at Harriet over his arm.

This time, Harriet laughed out loud. 'Oh, Will, you never stop, do you . . . I don't suppose you know what Gareth said to her?'

'They weren't on long. It was *my* mobile – so . . . She did say his shoulder's OK – better but not enough to come over.'

'Did she eat before she go to bed?' broke in Mme Dupont.

Will looked at her sharply. He shook his head. 'She was still a bit weepy,' he said. 'She just wanted to sleep. It seemed the best thing.'

Mme Dupont glanced at Harriet and shook her head.

'Will,' said Harriet, 'do you think – I mean – could I see her? Just for a minute or two? It's really very important.'

Will shook his head. 'Not a good idea, Harry. She's had enough for one day and so, may I say, have I.

She's OK. Jessica's fairly low-key at the moment too, if that's what's troubling you.'

'No. Not really. I know you'll take care of all that.'

'Oh, ta! Well, stop worrying your pretty little head and go home. And one day,' he said over his shoulder as he sashayed up the steps, 'you can tell me what all that rumpus was about at the theatre. But not now, dear heart, not now. I simply *must* do my hair . . .' And he flashed her a grin and a little wave of two fingers through the glass of the doors, to tell her that her outburst in the theatre was forgotten.

'Eh bien,' said Mme Dupont. ' 'E is a good boy.' Harriet nodded. 'But still she 'as not eaten.'

'No,' said Harriet. 'And I haven't told her—' But Mme Dupont had already started on the way back to the apartment. Harriet hurried after her. 'Will Mlle Cantal still be there?'

'Non, non, she will be back to zer theatre. It was not good fortune she come 'ome in between the shows today. She 'ardly ever do that – but, tant pis, too bad, it is done now. At least we 'ave Marianne safe.'

'Ye-e-es, but Mlle Cantal doesn't know that . . .' *Imagine going off to do a show when your daughter is missing,* thought Harriet.

'She trust me to find 'er,' said Mme Dupont. 'She

know Marianne will not go far, I t'ink. I will telephone and tell 'er.'

'She doesn't think it matters, Marianne being so thin?'

'Eh, bien. C'est comme ça, ma petite. It is like so. She want to be a ballerina 'erself when she was young. But she does not 'ave the – what you say – strength of will, hein? She cannot keep a diet.' Harriet nodded, remembering the cream, sugar and jam on the coffee tray. 'But that is not it. She did not 'ave the talent neither. Not that kind. She is good in shows, very good, but not for le ballet. And that break 'er 'eart. She is jealous of Marianne, I t'ink. But also, she want 'er to be a star.'

'It's a funny mixture,' said Harriet, 'wanting the two things at once. I don't really understand. Does she really – I mean, this seems an awful thing to say but – doesn't she love Marianne, just as she is? She seemed sort of, well . . . cold to her.'

Mme Dupont sighed. 'I t'ink she find it difficult – to love. Marianne try to please 'er but c'est jamais assez . . . it is never enough. Always there is something more she must do . . .'

'Poor Marianne.'

'Oui, poor Marianne.'

A small, sad frown on her face, Harriet walked

silently back to the apartment beside Mme Dupont, deep in thought. Always another mountain to climb to make your mother love you. No matter how good you were, how brilliant, how hard-working, you were never good enough, because your mother had some strange vision of what she wanted you to be. Something she had wanted for herself but could never do. How awful. And coming back to Paris for this performance would probably have made it worse. No wonder Marianne was ill. Well, she was safe in bed asleep now at least . . . But what about the morning, when all the work began again with still no food inside her? What then? Harriet knew that time was running out.

In the morning she awoke with a start. She scrambled out of bed and into the shower. She must get to the hostel before Marianne left for class and tell her what Giuseppina wanted her to know. But there was something else – suddenly, hot water tumbling down her back, her hair clinging to her face, she remembered . . . Lee Washington. How could she have forgotten? But she would miss his class if she went to see Marianne. Talking to her, telling her the whole story, trying to persuade her, would take so long . . .

Briskly she rubbed herself down. There was no contest. She was certain that with all the upset and no food for days, Marianne was likely to collapse. There was no time to waste. And she hadn't actually said to Lee that she'd be there today . . . or any day . . . but . . . As she rubbed herself dry, she thought longingly of the big studio with the black mirrored walls, the rhythm of the percussion, of working with professional dancers like Rosalie . . . Maybe there'd be a chance to go to Lee's class tomorrow. When she'd talked to Marianne . . .

Mme Dupont fussed a little about her going off on her own, but Harriet knew the way to the hostel, to the Opéra, she could even have got herself to Studio Goncourt if necessary, and she wanted to see Marianne alone. Marianne would probably be the one person in the world who would believe the story of Giuseppina. That photograph back in the school library *had* moved when Marianne was looking at it, Harriet was certain of it now. And Marianne had run away then, just as now she was running away from the truth. She would have run away from Giuseppina if she had seen her in the theatre. So Giuseppina had come to her, Harriet, to be her messenger.

She set off for the hostel. A wrong turning wasted precious minutes and when she finally got there, she found that the students had already left for the theatre. She ran through the streets, her rucksack banging about on her back, arriving breathless at the stage door. She hesitated. How was she to get into the theatre without being seen? But the television was still braying loudly from the concierge's room and she slipped past, keeping a keen eye open for staff or other students – *well, Jessica to be exact*, she thought – who might tell someone she was there.

At the bottom of the shadowy stairs up to the studio she paused again. In the distance, way above, she could hear the piano starting pliés already. Class had begun. She was too late to see Marianne now, she'd have to wait till class was over. And then what? How would she get past Miss McGregor and Alistair and everyone when she wasn't supposed to be here at all? She dumped herself down on the bottom stair, her head in her hands. She hadn't seen Marianne and she'd missed Lee's class for nothing.

Perhaps she should just let it go. Surely someone would see, would understand just how ill Marianne had become? If only Gareth were here to share all this. But he wasn't. There was just her. And Giuseppina ... Suddenly she lifted her head, listening ... Somewhere in the theatre other music was playing louder than the distant piano, the two sounds mixed up and discordant. She stood up and quietly started to climb the stairs.

At the pass-doors to the stage, she stopped, opened them a crack and listened. She'd heard aright. An orchestra was playing the Grand Pas de Deux from the last act of *Coppélia*. Giuseppina must be there. She slid through the door and into the wings.

The theatre was in darkness. A single spotlight skimmed and darted round the vast stage, following the movements of an invisible dancer. Harriet peered across at the opposite wing, but there was no one. No hand on the velvet curtain. No figure in the shadows. No one there and no one on stage. Just a moving light that dipped and guttered and the music fading away . . .

'Giuseppina, I know you're there somewhere. I'll tell her. I will – as soon as I can. I'll tell her . . .'

Harriet's whisper echoed round the huge space, bouncing off the walls and the distant ceiling, but all that came in reply was the vestige of a sigh from the darkness. The spotlight flickered and died. Silence.

Harriet groped her way out of the pass-door. No matter what, she would stand her ground, she would see Marianne, she would tell someone, anyone, that Marianne must have help and soon. But on the landing she stopped. Above her she heard anxious voices calling out, a door banging and feet rushing down towards her.

With a terrible premonition that she was too late, she flattened herself against the wall.

'Will?'

'Marianne! She's collapsed. I'm getting the concierge to call an ambulance.' And he disappeared past her, leaping three at a time down the stairs.

# Chapter 15

Harriet raced up the stairs and peered into the studio through the glass. Marianne lay on the floor by the barre, Miss Esbester kneeling beside her, Miss McGregor standing over her. She was covered in sweaters, towels, even leg warmers. The rest of the students huddled together in uneasy groups looking down at her, some wrapped up in their sweatshirts and wool-ups, talking quietly, others stretching gently at the barre to keep warm, Jessica among them. But Harriet noticed that even she stopped and looked over at Marianne every now and again, her face troubled.

Harriet watched for several long moments, shifting edgily from foot to foot. Surely Marianne would stir soon, come round, get herself up . . . but she went on lying there, unmoving, her face a ghastly white patch on the black surface of the floor. Miss Esbester looked up at Miss McGregor, shaking her head, looking really worried. Without stopping to take off her trainers, almost without thinking, Harriet burst into the studio, slipped between the two teachers and knelt beside Marianne.

'Harriet, what are you doing here? I thought I told you—', said Miss McGregor.

'Oh, please,' said Harriet. 'Please let me stay with her. Please don't make me . . .' She looked up at Miss Esbester. 'She needs a hospital, doesn't she?'

Miss Esbester nodded.

'Will she be – will they be able to . . . ?'

'I hope so, Harriet. I don't know. I hadn't realized, and I usually notice these things – so it can't have been all that long that she's not been eating . . . but she needs help.'

Miss McGregor sighed impatiently. 'Look, can you cope with this? I have to get on with the class. I can't stop everything for – I mean, we've other students and the matinée and . . .'

'Of course,' said Miss Esbester. She gave a brief smile. 'The show must go on,' she said with a lift of one eyebrow. 'Don't worry. The ambulance won't be long and Harriet can stay with me. I'll see there are no problems.' She gave a meaningful glance at Harriet. Miss McGregor was about to argue the point, but looked at the students round about her and let it go.

'Marianne isn't injured. I think we could move her very carefully,' said Miss Esbester, getting to her feet. With that, Will came barging back into the studio.

'Ambulance on its way,' he said.

'Thank you, Will.' Miss McGregor ran her hand over her head and down the back of her neck, and let out a breath. 'Boys, can you help Miss Esbester? But for goodness sake be careful. There's a small rest room just up the corridor . . .'

Miss Esbester led the way and Will and two or three other boys gently lifted Marianne and carried her from the studio. Harriet had a sudden terrible picture of a little coffin borne across a desolate square . . . She followed them out, loaded with odd garments that had dropped from Marianne when they picked her up. Behind her she heard Miss McGregor clap her hands, calling out the next exercise in an extra-strong voice, getting the class back together.

In the little room, the boys laid Marianne on a shabby couch and disappeared back to class, Will with a worried backward glance. Harriet sat beside Marianne. She took her hand, limp and frail, feeling the bones like the little white claws of a bird.

'Marianne! Marianne!' she said, quietly. Miss Esbester patted her shoulder.

'I'd let her be if I were you, Harriet,' she said. 'Better leave it to the ambulancemen.' She rummaged in her handbag, took out a list and ran a finger down it. 'I'll have to phone her father. And her mother is in Paris, isn't she? Her number isn't here.'

Harriet nodded. 'I've got it here somewhere,' she said, diving into her bag. 'It's where I'm staying.' As she took out her address book, her hand brushed against the book of photographs . . . Giuseppina's book . . .

'I'll go and phone from the office,' said Miss Esbester. 'It's only just up the corridor. I won't be long, but fetch me if you need me.' She looked down at Marianne, still and pale, wrapped in the bundles of clothes, and tucked a sweatshirt round her more firmly.

As Miss Esbester left the room, Harriet said, 'She will be all right, won't she? I mean – she's – she's not going to . . .'

'I don't think so, Harriet,' said Miss Esbester, 'but she's pretty ill. I don't know how she's managed to keep going all this week. And she'll have to co-operate with whatever treatment they advise, you know, or she'll be back where she started. That's very often quite a problem. And even if she does, she has to stick with it, and that's another.'

Harriet nodded. 'Yes. I understand,' she said. The forest in which Marianne was lost was deep and dark and there was no easy way out.

'Marianne,' she whispered urgently, 'Marianne . . .' But there was no reply. Marianne didn't stir. There was no way of reaching her, no way of giving her the message from Giuseppina. Except, maybe . . .

Harriet raced out of the room, down the stairs to the pass doors and plunged through them. She ran out on to the darkened stage not caring who saw her.

'Giuseppina!' she yelled, 'Giuseppina, please come. She's upstairs and I can't make her hear. But she might hear *you*! Please come! Please, please come!'

She wheeled frantically from wing to wing, wringing her hands, but nothing happened – and she had left Marianne alone. With a quick, desperate shake of her head, she turned and ran, leaving a black-garbed technician holding a stage light, open-mouthed.

Back at Marianne's side, she knelt down taking her fragile little hand in her own, trying to chafe it into life, but Marianne didn't move and the room was still. Harriet dropped her head in despair. Giuseppina hadn't come. Perhaps it was stupid to have thought she might. But at least she had tried. Now there was nothing more she could do. Two big tears ran down her cheeks.

But suddenly, Marianne stirred. Her eyelids flickered and her fingers convulsed as if she was trying to clutch at Harriet but hadn't the strength. Harriet brushed her hand across her face and leant forward eagerly.

'Marianne?' she whispered. For a moment there was silence and then the dry, cracked lips moved.

'I'm here, Marianne . . .' said Harriet again. 'I'm listening.'

'Giu— Giu—'

Giuseppina? Could that possibly be what she was saying?

'Giu— Giuse—' Marianne's breath came quickly. Harriet closed her eyes in relief. Yes . . . she had said Giuseppina. She looked up, but there was no one there. Giuseppina hadn't come, but now she could give Marianne the message herself.

'Hush, Marianne,' she said. 'It's all right. I think I know what you're trying to say. It's Giuseppina, isn't it? Giuseppina.' She held her breath.

Marianne gave a single, feeble nod. 'Giuseppina,' she whispered. 'Stay. Don't leave me . . .'

'Oh but I'm not . . .' said Harriet urgently. 'Of course I won't leave you. But, Marianne, I'm Harry.

I'm not Giuseppina, but I know what she wants to say to you . . .'

But Marianne tossed fretfully, pulling her hand away with sudden force and struggling to sit up. 'Stay with me . . . I'm listening . . .' She raised her hand. It dropped heavily but, almost as if someone had taken it and was lifting it for her, she raised it again.

In a panic, Harriet went to ease Marianne back on to the pillows. Marianne's eyes fluttered open, but Harriet knew they weren't seeing her, but something, someone far beyond her . . . and suddenly she understood. Giuseppina *was* there. Only Marianne could see her now, but she was there in this dingy room.

'No,' she said. 'No, she won't leave you. She's been with you all the time. All the time . . .' and she stepped away from the couch. Marianne smiled and struggled up, her eyes closed again. Slowly she placed her hands in front of her and they started to revolve round each other . . . *'dance . . . dancer . . .'* but she was too weak. She took a deep, shuddering breath. Up came her hands again, slowly, trembling. She passed them to and fro in front of her . . . *'must not . . . do not want'*. They dropped, but with a supreme effort she raised them a third time in fists above her head, brought them down in front of her one above the other, and fell back. '*Death* . . .'

'Giuseppina,' she said faintly, and then was quiet.

Horribly quiet. Harriet took her hand and held it tightly, for a moment touching it to her cheek. It was cold . . . very cold. Behind her she heard heavy footsteps coming up the stairs. Within moments she was ushered unceremoniously out of the room while the ambulancemen and Miss Esbester gathered round the couch, and Marianne was lifted up and taken away.

'Only one person in the ambulance I'm afraid, Harriet,' Miss Esbester had said, 'and that has to be me. But I spoke to a Mme Dupont, who will be at the hospital to meet us. Marianne's mother is – indisposed it appears, and this good lady looks after Marianne when she is in Paris.'

Harriet had nodded, relieved that Mme Dupont would be in charge.

'Now,' Miss Esbester had continued, 'I'll have to get back for rehearsals and anyway, it's best if it's her family with her. You can visit her later, I hope.' She had given Harriet a straight look and said, 'You'll have to stay here, Harriet, so . . . no trouble . . .'

Harriet said, 'Of course not,' indignantly, and with

a little smile, Miss Esbester had gone with Marianne.

But, sitting on a bench on the landing outside the studio, Harriet was in an agony of doubt and anxiety. If Marianne had really seen Giuseppina, what did that mean? She had thought Giuseppina's message was to help Marianne. But had she been wrong . . . had she misunderstood? Did it really mean she had come – come to fetch Marianne? To take her away for ever – that Marianne would die? She thought of that last weak, hesitant gesture . . . Miss Esbester might think she was going to be all right, but supposing . . .

Suddenly Alistair came running up the stairs, out of breath, looking upset and worried. He dashed into the studio, interrupting class. Unashamed, Harriet jumped up, put her ear to the doors and listened.

'What's all this now?' he practically yelled.

'Oh, Alistair, I'm so sorry.' That was Miss McGregor. 'Just come outside for a moment . . .' The music stopped and Harriet heard a low mutter from the students. She slid back on to the bench just in time as the door opened. Miss McGregor turned back and said to the pianist, 'Roy, just take that exercise through again for them, will you? I won't be a minute.' The piano started again. Not noticing Harriet squashed up on the bench, Miss McGregor grasped Alistair's arm.

'Alistair, I don't know what to say. But Marianne's gone to hospital. There's no way she can dance on Saturday.'

'But – oh God, after all that *work* . . .'

'I know. I'm so sorry . . .'

'I really wanted it to – I mean, I know there were problems, but it would – she would have been all right on the day, I'm sure she would.'

'She's too ill, Alistair. She's not going to be dancing for quite a while. What do you want to do? Can we put Jessica on?'

Harriet's head jerked up. Jessica? Oh no, not that . . . But Alistair was shaking his head.

'I don't think so. She's not right for it . . . not really. She knows it. I mean she can get through it, but that's not the point. I think it would be best to cancel. I'd rather not do it than have it done badly and I don't think she . . .'

Harriet sat very still, looking up at Alistair, one hand leaning forwards on to the wall, his head on his arm, tapping the toes of one foot behind him, his face creased up with disappointment.

'We'd better tell Will,' said Miss McGregor.

Alistair looked up and nodded. 'I guess so,' he said, and dropped his head again. Miss McGregor looked into the studio and beckoned.

Harriet stiffened. What about Will? Look at all he'd done. He'd done so much – he'd been . . . And Jessica? Even Jessica couldn't crow over Marianne now, not now she was as ill as this. And perhaps – perhaps with Marianne not there to make her jealous, insecure maybe, whatever it was that made her so – so awful sometimes, perhaps she'd be better in the pas de deux. Not perfect, not Marianne, but all right. And it would give Will the chance . . .

Will came out, rubbing his neck with a towel, but when he saw Alistair he stopped, his face falling.

'Oh,' he said. 'That's it, then. We're not going to do it . . . She's too sick.'

Alistair nodded. 'That's about it, Will,' he said. 'I'm sorry.'

Will sighed. After a moment, he shrugged and held up his hands. ' 'Nother day, 'nother dollar,' he said brightly, but his jaw was working and Harriet could tell that inside, he was choked. He turned away to go back into class, his shoulders drooping, even his purple highlights subdued. Harriet took her courage in both hands and stood up.

'Please, Alistair,' she said in a small voice. 'Couldn't you let Jessica just try? Will's worked so hard. And if anyone can manage Jessica he can. She might be all right with Marianne not here. You know, no one to get one over, no one to – to *beat* . . .'

Miss McGregor rounded on her. 'What are you doing here, Harriet?' she said, angrily. 'I thought I told you . . . Haven't you done enough damage?'

But Alistair kicked a little harder at the ground, pursing his lips. 'I'd really like to see it go on,' he said, 'here of all places . . . and it's true, Will, you should have a go, it's only right. You've worked – you've worked really well . . . Been a bit of a hero really . . .' He prodded the ground a little more with his toes and then pushed himself upright, slapping the wall.

'Let's give it a try,' he said. 'As soon as class is over, we'll give it a go. If it doesn't work, then we take it out, but – but it's worth a try. OK, Will?'

Will rubbed his neck vigorously and gave a big grin. 'Great,' he said.

'Very well,' said Miss McGregor. 'I'll tell Jessica. I'm sure she'll do her best,' and looking quite pleased, she went back into the studio. Alistair turned and went down the stairs towards the stage.

'See you in fifteen, Will,' he called up the stairwell.

'OK,' called Will, leaning over the rail. He turned to Harriet. 'Harry, dear heart – you're not all bad.' He flung an arm round her shoulder and squeezed. 'Thank you, that was really very – well, very *brave*,' he said, and dabbed at his face with his towel.

Harriet smiled. 'I won't tell Marianne till it's over though,' she said. 'Just in case she gets out of bed and—' She stopped short, anxiety for Marianne taking over.

'Listen,' said Will, 'La Marianna will be all right. She's not stupid, Harry. Missing the pas de deux will be enough to make her see straight.'

'Hope so.' Harriet wasn't convinced. She knew that it wasn't a question of being stupid. 'Did you know?'

'Hmm. I sort of guessed. You can't partner someone, especially someone new, without noticing. But I thought we'd get through the performance and then maybe . . .'

Harriet nodded. 'That's what *we* thought, Gareth and me. We should have told you.'

'Well . . . oh, never mind, eh . . . Listen, I'd better get ready for the next part of this cantata. Jessica, huh? Grit the teeth and carry on . . .' He flashed a grin, baring his teeth and gnashing them together, and Harriet laughed.

'Go on,' she said, 'you'll love it.' Then, as he turned to go, she looked at his hair. 'Umm – just what colour are you going to do the hair for the little cantata? It can't stay that colour.'

'Red, white and blue,' he said firmly, 'the in colour for heroes – what else?' and with a flick of his shoulder he pushed through the doors. Harriet laughed. A likely story, even for Will, though it had an appeal. She turned at the sound of Miss Esbester coming up the stairs. She ran down to meet her.

'How is she?'

'She's come round. They're putting her on a drip and all that sort of thing, but she'll be all right. Her father is coming to take her back to England for treatment there. And there's a taxi waiting downstairs to take you to the hospital. Mme Dupont insisted. You can't see Marianne till this evening, but you'll be near her and Mme Dupont said she would be happier to have you close by.' Her eyes twinkled at Harriet. 'I can't imagine why, but at least you won't be in everyone's way here. So off you go.'

With a grin, Harriet grabbed her rucksack, ran downstairs, past the concierge's room, and out into the taxi.

'I saw 'er . . .'

Marianne lay in the little hospital room, still looking waif-like and all bones, tubes coming from just about everywhere it seemed, but already with a little colour in her cheeks.

'Giuseppina? Yes, I thought you did.'

She nodded. 'In that little room à l'Opéra. She came and told me – about how she had danced Swanilda and then got sick and died. So nearly a great ballerina, dancing all the big roles, in all the books like Pavlova and Fonteyn, but then . . .' She turned her head sadly and drowsily towards Harriet. 'She didn't want – she didn't want it to happen to me. Pauvre Giuseppina. She couldn't help what happened to her, when all the guns came and the terrible sickness . . . but I could – I could . . .'

Harriet nodded. That was the message. *'Giuseppina died. Tell Marianne she must not die. She must dance.'* The message she would have given Marianne if she could have reached her in time.

' 'Arry, I kind of knew when I saw the photograph move in the library. I knew she wanted to tell me something, but I didn't want to 'ear . . . I run – ran away.'

Harriet smiled. 'And you kept on running. Never mind. You know now.'

'Yes. I know now. And I won't let it 'appen to me. I promised 'er.'

Mme Dupont put her head round the door and beckoned. Harriet nodded. She delved into her rucksack, brought out a bedraggled, faded silk flower and laid it gently on the bed beside Marianne.

'I think Giuseppina would like you to have this,' she said.

'It belonged to 'er?' said Marianne. ' 'Ow did you—?'

'It's a long story,' said Harriet. 'I'll tell you one day. But I have to go now. Mme Dupont's waiting and you're tired. But I'm sure she'd want you to have it.'

When she looked back, Marianne was holding the flower close to her cheek, her eyes closed, sleeping peacefully.

Tomorrow, Marianne would go back to England with her father. Harriet was to go too. There was to be a nurse with them and another hospital waiting. But first there was something very important Harriet had to do. She scribbled a note for dear, lovely Mme Dupont to leave for Lee Washington.

'Non, non, ma petite, I will not *leave* it. I will give it to him moi-même – mine self.' And no doubt she would. Quite what Lee Washington would make of her, Harriet smiled to think. Perhaps she'd do high kicks for him. He'd probably enjoy that.

She wished she could be there.

But one day, one day she *would* be there. She would dance with him, or if not him, then someone like him. The world was full of people to dance with, exciting new ways to dance she'd never dreamt of. Rosalie was right, there *was* life after swans.

But in the meantime, there were classes to do, things to learn, there was even a project to finish. She looked down at Giuseppina's photograph in the book lying on Marianne's little bed. She was definitely kneeling the right way round now, her tulle fluffed out round her, the white hands crossed, the ringlets tumbling, the dark eyes modestly downcast towards the bouquet on the floor at her feet in their strange soft little shoes. Everything as it should be . . . except that perhaps the bouquet was not quite as big as it had once been . . .

She closed the book carefully and put it in the bottom of her rucksack, packing the rest of her few bits and pieces on top of it, ready to go home. Marianne's father was waiting in his car. She sighed. Yes, it was true there was life after swans, but for now it was enough that there was life at all . . .

She gave Mme Dupont the hug to end all hugs, hoiked her rucksack on her shoulder, gave it a pat and went out of the door.

# A note from the author

The story of Giuseppina and her brief rise to fame is true. The eminent writer on ballet history, Ivor Guest, tells it in his book *The Ballet of the Second Empire*, where you will also find photographs of Giuseppina and other dancers of her time. You will probably have to ask your local library for the book as it is quite old now.

There are several versions of Giuseppina's story. In some, smallpox is given as the cause of her death, but others suggest that it was cholera, which was rife in Paris in the siege of 1870. Once the siege began and the Opéra closed, Giuseppina was poverty-stricken, living with her family at No. 20 Passage Saulnier, described as 'a dark apartment in a sad house'.

Giuseppina's funeral was a much grander affair than the way I have described it in *Harriet's Ghost*. She was attended by dancers and singers from the Opéra and three rows of white marguerites were planted by her open grave in the cemetery at Montmartre. In a funeral speech, a Director of the Opéra said: 'Poor dear child! All the brilliance of her youth, her budding beauty, that blossoming of all gifts and all charms . . . are buried for ever in this pitiless coffin . . . May these flowers, these last pale flowers of this fateful year, lie close and whisper our farewell. These pure emblems of candour, youth and innocence can be no more chaste, no more immaculate, than was the charming being who is today no more than a memory, and who bore the name – Giuseppina Bozzacchi.'

On a simple wooden cross her name was inscribed with the words 'Étoile de l'Opéra', Star of the Opéra, but the inscription faded very soon afterwards, leaving no trace.

## STEP INTO THE DARK

*Bridget Crowley*

*The eerily-lit staircase seemed to hide not ghosts, but things and people that meant terrible harm. The balcony in the Hall seemed far away, like a beautiful dream he had to wake up from. Reality was home and getting up to the ninth floor unscathed.*

Danger surrounds Beetle wherever he is. When he tries to protect Tamar, the beautiful young singer, he becomes a target for the bullies' violent games. And then there's the girl in white, who vanishes as mysteriously as she appears. Could she be a ghost – and if she is, why is she calling out to Beetle across the darkness . . . ?

'A highly likeable and accomplished first novel . . . briskly paced without being rushed, the story will engage readers with its real sense of urban teenage life.' Linda Newbery, *Times Educational Supplement*